*Blind Man and The Bimbo*

by Paul Anders
*35,000 words*
*ISBN 978-0-9841603-2-7*

To obtain permissions, write *support@zanybooks.com*

To purchase more fine books like the one you're reading, go to *http://zanybooks.com*.

Chapter 1

The smells of newly cut grass and horse dung from the track nearby mingle with the tang of Eucalyptus and the occasional heady whiff of pine. The air, for once, is free of tobacco fumes and the music, loud and raucous, promises heavy doings in the evening ahead.

The Big Hoss Dance Hall outdoors next to the Santa Anita Race Track is well worth the extra half-hour's drive, and I hoped by now Girl had regained some of her normal good temper.

"I want to dance," I said to her, "Who've we got?"

"Buxom blond, maybe too buxom, wearing stretch pants."

"You know how I feel about …"

She pressed on ignoring me, "Foxy brunette, tall, slim … no, forget that one, she and her partner are wearing matching outfits, probably married. Now here's an odd one."

Girl's hand shifted on my arm and I could hear the faint whisper of her fingers running through her hair. The sound was accompanied by the delicate odor of perfume, shampoo, and Girl herself. This odd one must be competition, and competition do make Girl nervous.

"The woman's in her mid-thirties, I'm guessing, short dark hair, her partner's just a teenager."

"Little short fellow?" My voice, deep as a nighttime disk jockey's, could have belonged to a news anchorman, but was just the speech of a once-upon-a-time professor of anatomy.

Girl's voice was deep too, for a girl, and resonant—she'd sung in a choir in high school, and still did when she went to church. "No, he's quite tall, towers over his mom. That's probably what it is, mother and son."

"Bad idea for her to dance with him. Give the kid an Oedipus complex—if he doesn't have one already. I'd better dance with her, give the child a chance to strike out on his own."

Girl laughed, amused rather than impressed by my logic. She continued with her summary of the passing crowd and, a moment later, called out to someone walking nearby. I stood mechanically as Girl took my wrist and placed a small feminine hand in mine.

"You're...?"

"Brigitte."

"I know a Brigitte." I began.

"I'm the one," Brigitte announced and giggled.

Yes, I knew a Brigitte all right: short, red hair—almost orange I'd been told; she smelled good, real good. But she giggled, wore too much hand lotion, and had no real sense of the music. Why had Girl stuck me with her? What had happened to the brunette? One dance, that was all I'd give this Brigitte.

"Oh, dance this next one with me," Brigitte said, "you know I love the cha-cha."

So do I. "I'd like to but I promised Girl."

"Why do you call her Girl? Her name is Marci."

"What's the point of learning their names? They never stay around long enough, none of them have, not since the... explosion." There, I could say the word now, didn't really bother me anymore.

Brigitte's temper was in keeping with her red hair. She raised her voice to tell me what I already knew. "Maybe they'd stay around longer if you were nicer. Maybe if you were really nice, you could find someone permanent to live with you, you wouldn't have to hire a girl."

Like you, I thought, with your permanent smell of honey, and hand lotion, and fresh salt air. And that dammed giggle.

3

We'd stopped on the edge of the dance floor to talk; the other dancers whirled by inches from us; the long skirts of one brushed my pant leg. For an instant, I felt an intense sadness.

I should have danced the cha-cha. Would have shut Brigitte up. Damned conversation with these women never leads anywhere.

"Get me a dancer this time," I begged Girl.

"I'm trying." she said, "Brigitte was a volunteer, she likes you. Some of the women find you ill-tempered, not her. Trouble with you is you're so fussy, they're always 'too short,' or 'tries to lead.'

"I'll tell you something, Professor Anders. At this particular out-of-the-way dance place you insisted we come to tonight, 'can't stand the smoke,' you said, 'want fresh air,' they're either all married, or they don't know how to do anything but line dance."

"What about the brunette? The one with the kid?"

"So far she hasn't let go of him. Wait, I see her doing Slapping Leather. A couple of minutes from now could be your big opportunity."

"It will be if you get your big butt over there."

Girl got; at least she got out of range of what remains of my poor vision. As always, I felt helpless when she was out of earshot.

"Redneck Girl," went the tune. What other kind was there?

Returning bootsteps and multiple silhouettes said Girl had been at least partially successful; I just hoped it wasn't another damned Brigitte.

"This is Donna Clark and her son Greg. I'm going to dance with Greg, maybe you could entertain Donna."

But I had already taken Donna's hand and was leading her out onto the dance floor. What did I want to be introduced to the son for? He was probably as cute as a dancing bear.

Donna Clark said her son was only 13 and well on his way to being a competition dancer. "I spend most of my free time taking him to and from dance lessons. He taught me to dance, the west-coast swing anyway."

Touch told me Donna wore a short-sleeved blouse with fringe on the shoulders, jeans with a braded leather belt, and boots. She was slim, each of her ribs sharp and definite against the skin, hips not much wider than mine; she smelled of sunflowers.

"You're a good dancer," she said, the light puff of her breath against my cheek suggesting she'd just been eating peaches.

Slow, slow, quick, quick, I said inwardly in time with the music. I took a deep breath, wondering what I could say aloud in reply. "It's easy to dance with you, too. You're so very light on your feet."

"Thank you," she said and rested her head against my shoulder for a brief intoxicating moment. "I've seen you before," she confided. "In Cahoots in Fullerton."

"I'm a Wednesday night regular; Saturdays too, if I haven't got a date." Slow, slow, quick, quick.

"I usually go Saturdays," she said.

"Be there tomorrow?" I asked, trying to sound calm and unemotional.

"I might be." She sounded uncertain rather than flirtatious; not at all the commitment I wanted her to make. "I should go check on Greg. My son," she added when she saw his name was still a mystery to me.

She left me, and I wished my eyes could follow her across the floor. I wondered if I'd dance with Donna again.

I danced with Girl; we dance well together—she stands at 5'11," an inch taller than I am, so we truly dance cheek to cheek—but her heart is never really in it. As with my own daughters, she seems distracted, as if her eyes are constantly darting about the room appraising, searching for someone her own age.

After making sure that I had the retaining wall of a planter at my back and was out of the way of traffic, Girl drifted away on some mysterious errand. Probably she had found that someone, or at least someone who would do for a dance or three.

I waited patiently, not dancing, as cooler air crept down from the San Gabriel Mountains. It was getting late; we probably should be on our way. "Girl!" Where the hell was she anyway? Someone about Girl's height stood a few feet from where I sat by the planter, had been standing there for some time. I'd assumed it was Girl. Then, why didn't she answer?

"Who are you?" I demanded.

"Me, Sir?" An adolescent's voice, unsteady, oscillating between a boy's and a man's.

"Yes, you."

"Greg. I'm Greg. I was looking for my mother. She was dancing with you earlier."

"I thought she'd gone home."

"We were supposed to half an hour ago; I can't find her," the kid said, whining. Grow up kid. Life is tough.

"Check the rest rooms. I could send Girl to look. If she were here that is."

"I am here," came that fresh young voice from off to my right, "and the name is Marci."

"Girl," I snapped.

"Marci. But don't worry; you'll get it right sooner or later, Professor. You want to go home I suppose."

"No, I'm planning to spend the night. First, we'll find the young man's mother."

"I thought you two were together," Girl said to Greg. He kicked the side of the planter with his foot, hesitated. "I was dancing with Barbara; she likes to do the west coast swing.

When I came back my mother was gone. She said this would be the last dance." The boy's voice descended in an instant from suave maturity to helplessness, and finished on a note of despair.

"She's got to be here," Girl said, "They're shooing people out toward the gates."

"I'll find her," I announced, and started back across the dance floor. We couldn't all afford to be helpless.

"They've turned off the lights."

"Not a problem." For me it wasn't a problem. Not anymore, I was always in the dark now.

"Where are you going?" Girl called out behind me as I started up the stairs to the racetrack proper. The answer should have been obvious, though I forbore from telling her so. If the boy's mother wasn't on the dance floor and wasn't in the rest room, then she had to have gone out to the track. I often do when I find a willing female; the darkness is romantic as hell, and the San Gabriel Mountains in the background seem to have an erotic effect.

I could hear them clattering up the stairs behind me. A man's voice cried out, "You can't go in there. Closed." Ignoring the voice, I continued to thread my way across the linoleum floor. For an instant, I lost my balance—I'd stepped on a discarded racing program, but then I was back outside again, with only the track and the mountains ahead of me.

I had to be careful now; the occasional stair interrupted the ramp leading downward. Behind me were the sounds of a generator. Off to the right: voices, two men and a woman. Not a conversation, an argument.

A figure loomed ahead of me out of the darkness; I stopped, giving him or her a chance to go around me.

"Where do you think you're going?" a man's voice challenged. "We're trying to be alone here."

"Tell him to fuck off," a second male voice, deeper than the first, instructed from the shadows.

"Donna?" I ventured. If I were wrong, I'd just have to fuck off; if I were right, well, hopefully, Girl and the boy were right behind me.

From ahead of me in the darkness by the railing, Donna's clear resonant voice asked, "Professor? What are you doing out here?" She sounded relieved rather than inquisitive.

"Greg sent me to get you."

"Thank you. I was just telling Frank, Greg would be worrying about me."

"Both of you shut the fuck up," the deeper male voice, Frank's, instructed. "Professor, whoever you are, go away. We got business to discuss. Tell the brat his momma will be there when she gets there."

The shadow of the other man pushed against me, and I'd just locked his arm and elbow in a push-me, pull-me hold when Girl, Greg, and a puffing security person finally arrived. Why do sighted people have so much difficulty getting around in the dark?

"Put on the damn lights," puffed the guard who'd been chasing us.

"We're not supposed to," whined a fifth person, a custodian presumably.

"All of you get out of here," Frank said.

The second man, still bent over in the half-crouch where I'd twisted him, tugged on his arm. I let go of him and a grunt announced his hitting the row of chairs behind. He lay on the concrete for a moment, rubbing his arm, presumably, and muttered something about that "damned blind man."

Donna chose that moment to link her arms with Greg and I, and to march us away from the discussion. I felt eminently proud of myself. Donna's breath, redolent of peaches, was again in my ear. "Thank you."

## Chapter 2

"Donna's a very pretty girl," I said to get the conversational ball rolling.

Girl and I had sat in almost total silence since we'd slipped into my new Volvo sports coupe. (Total protection plus enough engine to power through a twenty-car pileup. Perhaps, this was like locking the barn door after the bull was stolen; I hadn't the insurance money to spend on such necessities before.)

We'd packed Donna and Greg safely away in their ancient Toyota—I'd insisted on doing that before we left; I'd stayed quiet out of respect for my driver through the slalom course that was the exit from the race track, had endured a mile or so of the fragrant duck farm that marks the first few miles of the freeway south, but enough was enough. Half the fun in going places with a companion is talking about it with them afterward.

"I told Donna we'd be at In Cahoots tomorrow," I added. What was Girl so uptight about anyway?

Her staccato reply took me off guard. "What makes you think we'll be at In Cahoots? I do get days off; it's in my contract." She slapped the steering wheel indignantly. "What makes you think Donna will be there? Besides, she's not right for you."

What had gotten into my not-so-little buddy? "Are you jealous?"

Girl snorted and twisted about on the genuine leather seat, making a sound like escaping gas. "For one thing, she's half your age."

"You're half my age." I scored one that time.

"If you were ten years younger."

"Five."

Ooh was she angry. Girl flipped on the radio, hunted for a station and found Yani's music to ride elevators by, which I knew she disliked almost as much as I do.

In less than half a record ("White Christmas?" "Get By With a Little Help From My Friends?" "Sail Away?" hard to tell with that kind of beat) she flipped the radio off again. "I'll take you to In Cahoots," she said, "but you won't be happy, that woman will be all kinds of trouble. Besides, she has no hips."

Hmm, now that was something to think about.

The next night, we went to In Cahoots. I knew we would, never had the slightest doubt of it. Girl knows almost as many dancers as I do. Both of us are shaking hands or exchanging hugs almost as soon as we walk through the door. Never mind that her age group doesn't really show up until mine is leaving. Enough in-betweens are always present to keep us both happy.

I wore my black outfit: black denim jeans, black Pierre Cardon shirt, and big silver belt buckle with my initials in raised lettering. Too hot to wear a hat; besides, women like hair they can run their fingers through.

It looked to be a two-dance night. On a three-dance night, a Monday, say, I'd pretty much dance with the same girl until they played a line dance or something, and then I'd get me a new partner after I sat a dance or so out. On a one-dance night, a couple of super-crowded Fridays each month, too many willing partners make it impossible to spend more than one dance with any of them. This Saturday evening was somewhere in between. Brigitte again, and Sally, and Kim, Mary, Marie, and Maria. (The Mary and the Marie are actually best friends; can you believe it?)

First west coast swing of the evening, I danced with Girl. The next, somebody took my hand and said with the slight lilt of Tennessee, "Could I have the pleasure?' Donna had shown up after all.

She wore a long-sleeved blouse with fringe on the arms like the feathers on the wings of the Andean Condor and the same perfume she had worn the previous night. I felt as if I'd walked into a field of sunflowers. Each and every one smelled wonderful to me.

After the swing, we danced a waltz, a cha-cha, and a riding double. We got better and better as a couple each time we danced. I didn't think I'd be dancing with anyone else that evening, but "I'll be back," she told me before I could protest.

I spent a vacant half hour dancing with partners I didn't particularly care for, and then Donna was back in my arms again. I held her as closely as I thought I could get away with.

The interval had given me a chance to rehearse my speech: "I always go to Mile Square Park on Sundays," I said to her. "There's usually a concert scheduled. Will you come with me to the park tomorrow?"

"Sure," she said. "Although, I was kind of hoping you'd take me to..." Her voice died in the middle of the sentence.

"What did you want to do instead?"

"Well I was hoping you'd want to come here Sunday night, for the lesson." She squeezed my hand. "But that doesn't mean we can't also go to the park."

"We'll do both." I was surprised to find both my feet were still on the ground. If my feet had been true to my feelings, they'd have been dancing along the ceiling of the club.

She pulled closer and whispered in my ear. "Should I phone you tomorrow to work out the details? Or, I could write down my phone number and give it to Marci."

"You tell me your phone number," I countered, "and I'll memorize it." And for the next fifteen minutes, instead of slow, slow, quick, quick, I went 555–4711, over and over in time with the music.

"Who else is she dancing with?" I asked Girl during one of the breaks. By this time, I didn't have to explain who "she" was.

"That idiot who was holding her hostage last night at the track for one."

"You're kidding."

"But that was only the one time. She's danced with a lot of guys. She's a popular girl."

"You know why I like her?" I asked—I wasn't really changing the subject. "Last night at Big Hoss, she told me I was a good dancer."

Girl snorted.

"Not 'You're a good dancer for a blind guy.' Just, I was a good dancer."

"You are a good dancer."

"Then stop wondering what she sees in me."

And it was Girl's turn to hug me as tightly as she dared.

Chapter 3

I waited impatiently till ten the next morning before phoning.

Maybe calling so early wasn't a good idea; maybe Donna would think I was too eager, but I had to know if I really had a date with her. Despite my bravado on the ride home, the difference in our ages did concern me, and so did my lack of sight. What did I have to offer a woman like Donna? Security, I suppose, I'd put a good deal away before the accident, and we both liked to dance. She'd said I was a good dancer.

"Hello," her boy answered in a tentative, shaky voice.

"Hi, this is Paul Anders, we met two days ago at the Santa Anita Race Track."

The joyous "Hi" in reply did make it sound as if he were at least pleased I was calling, but he didn't say anything more and, for a moment, neither did I.

"Could I speak with your mother?"

"She's not home."

He didn't sound very happy about it. I decided to remain silent another moment or two to see if the silence would stimulate more of an admission. It did.

"She didn't come home last night."

Shit, and I'd been worried about coming on too strong. Some other guy had caught her. How does the old county song go: "I should have asked her faster."

"I'm worried," the boy, Greg said.

He was worried. I have kids too, had, (three daughters, youngest is 19, she lives in Seattle) and I recognized the tone. "Was she supposed to come home?"

"She didn't call." Again the note of desolation.

"Want me to come over there?"

"If you want to."

He wasn't too sure of the directions, few kids are, at least until they get their first driver's license. I got better results when I asked him what school he went to. "Marina," I repeated back to him. "That's just around the corner. I'll pick you up, then we'll go look for your mom."

"I could come to your house," he said, sounding more confident, "I've got a bicycle."

"Okay" Kid would probably get a kick out of riding his bicycle. I always did when I was his age. More important, with him riding his bicycle, I wouldn't have to wake Girl up to drive the car.

Figuring Greg might be hungry, I went into the kitchen and started fixing a second breakfast for the two of us. It was a lot like my first, only this time I skipped the orange juice and made herbal tea instead of coffee. I figured Greg would drink milk and hefted the carton to be sure there would be enough for him. Teenagers are fussy, but I knew he wouldn't object to that morning's main course—peanut butter sandwiches and granny smith apples.

His knock on the door came just as I was visualizing my own teen-age bicycling days, those endless rides through the neighborhood, always looking everywhere at once, hoping some girl might come out for just a moment on her porch.

"What's that jingling sound you make when you walk?" I asked.

"Wallet chain."

"No trouble finding the place?"

Hard to answer with your mouth full. Peanut butter, apple, and milk proved to be just what Greg had been hoping for. I don't doubt he could have fixed his own breakfast, he was 13 after all, but he probably had been too upset till then to stop to eat.

"Where do you think your mother is?" I asked him, when nothing was left but crumbs. "Has she been dating someone?"

Okay, so maybe that last question was for my benefit and not his. But she hadn't been dating anyone, Greg told me. "Frank?" This was the guy who'd been manhandling her at the racetrack. But he was just someone she'd met dancing, oh, and Frank knew Greg's Dad.

"Did you phone your Dad?" I asked, thinking her ex must be my real competition, if she hadn't gone back to him already.

Greg said he'd called his Dad, and his Dad wasn't home, which was odd, Greg said, "'cause he was supposed to be spending the afternoon with me."

"Do you want to go over to his place and look around?"

Greg pushed back his chair and stood up ready to go, so I guess the answer was "yes." Fed, with another person for company, and a definite plan of action, he was as excited as he'd been desolate and alone less than an hour before.

"We'll go to your Dad's place then. Can you drive?"

"Sorta."

I didn't like the sound of that "sorta," and debated waking Girl, but then thought no, she might just nix the whole idea. I mean, what business did I have chasing after Donna, anyway?

The drawback was I had no one to check my clothes. I didn't think I could trust Greg's judgment. Pulling my shirt from the green end of the closet, I reached for a pair of walking shorts. Hopefully, these were also green or brown, not blue.

"We've got to be quiet until we're out of here," I warned him, much as a hundred years before Tom Sawyer might have cautioned Huck Finn. "Don't make a sound till we're away from the apartments."

We made it undetected down the walk past my scented garden—rosemary, sage, all kinds of basils, and roses, to the carport. I was just showing Greg how to adjust the mirrors when Girl caught up with us.

"Where are you going?" she called out in that insufferably cheerful voice. For a kid that's had to overcome so many problems just to get the beginnings of a college education, you'd think she'd be a little less upbeat.

"Just the two of you, uh. Do you have a driver's license?" she asked Greg and not waiting for his mumbled, "No." added, "I suppose Professor Anders was going to take over when you reached the freeway."

"Weren't going to use the freeway," Greg said.

"Exactly. Well, why don't I drive then? Greg, you just pop in the back. I was going for a run, but seeing as you two are so eager, I'll come with you."

Judging from the tang of healthy young womanhood that joined me on the front seat, she'd already run several laps. I wondered what the appearance of her striking, near six-foot blond figure in a body glove would do to Greg's father.

Girl was a natural athlete, had competed in half a dozen sports in high school and would probably be on her college team if she didn't have me to squire around.

We'd met at the Aikido dojo, Aikido being one of the few sports I have remaining to me (other than running and swimming which in their self-induced isolation have always struck me as singularly depressing). I'd had the "pleasure" of working with Girl on her first day. Not her first day in Aikido, I discovered shortly, just her first day with my training group.

I began with a Front-Strike First Control at Sensei Segal's suggestion and was impressed with how rapidly she picked up the move. We went quickly in succession through most of the lower-belt exercises, when I finally deigned to exchange a few words. "I'm testing fourth," I said. "Looks like you could work with me."

"Glad to," she said not even puffing, and when she didn't offer her rank, I asked straight out, "What color is your belt?"

"Brown," she said, "I'm a third-degree brown." which meant she was something like five belts above me and could be testing black, if she wanted to. Testing black in Aikido means you're willing to devote your life to the training, and take vows of poverty or something. She was at the top as far as a civilian was concerned. "Thank you, Arigato," I said, bowing, and vowed to forever keep my mouth shut.

Later, when I learned she was looking for a job she could fit into her college schedule, I made her an offer. The next evening, she accepted. It's not a bad deal; she gets her own apartment, rent free—I own the whole building—and we arrange the hours so we're both satisfied. I just need to get to the store and the library once in a while (they have books on tape and CD's; too late for me to learn Braille) and in the evenings she'll take me to a concert or dancing, dropping me off if she has a date, then picking me up later.

Not everyone likes the idea of being dependent on a blind person's whim. She's the exception. Okay. I like her. I hope she likes me, too, and I can start thinking of her as a Marci instead of just another Girl.

Chapter 4

"Where are we going?" Marci asked after we'd been driving for a while, hopefully in the right direction.

"I'm not sure," Greg said, an answer that didn't surprise me. I wondered how the two of us alone would have gotten anywhere if he'd had to drive as well as navigate.

Artie Clark's place was located in an area where nobody had painted their home or cut the grass in a long, long time. If location was everything, this place had nothing. Or maybe it was Greg's father who was bringing down the neighborhood.

Artie's house could only be distinguished from its neighbors because it was a little more desolate, its door, according to Marci, more in need of a coat of paint. Lack of water had killed off most of what passed for a lawn. I was advised to bypass the cracked cement walk and make my way among the gopher holes.

Not even a lock on the door. I turned the handle and we were inside. Dust and mildew, drying paint: perhaps Artie was trying to make things better.

We made it to the kitchen guided by the smell.

"Someone's just cleaned up," Marci said.

The trashcan had been emptied, though an eggshell lay beside it on the floor, and the sink was clear of dishes. The refrigerator held a quart of milk—maybe Artie was expecting his son for the weekend—hot dogs, carrots and an apple.

"How long do you think he's been gone?" Marci asked.

"Day, couple of days at most; he might even have been here this morning. You can tell by the cooking odor.

"The phone's been disconnected." I turned to Greg accusingly, "I thought you said you phoned him."

"I did." His indignant adolescent voice climbed a full octave in protest.

The phone calls were being forwarded someplace else. Where? And why?

Girl and Greg were in the second smaller bedroom, where Greg had some of his things, when the light was suddenly cut off from the doorway. I looked up and saw an immense silhouette, like that of the offensive guard the man must have been back in high school.

Who the hell was he?

I stepped forward quickly, both to put him on the defensive and to give Girl and Greg a chance to stay out of the way. "Hi," I said, "How can I help you?"

"Artie Clark?" he questioned in response to my touch. His arm could have been cut from the trunk of a small tree.

"Not here. How can I help you?" I repeated.

Greg, alas, chose that moment to come out of the bedroom. "I can't find—" he began and stopped when he saw the big man. "Who are you?" Greg said, "Do you know where my father is?"

So much for my plan to tell the big one I was Greg's father.

"I'm Lionel," the man said. "I'm looking for your Dad, too." He brushed past me and headed for Greg. Was he going to hurt him? I felt about me for something I might use to lure the big man close with. The only objects that came easily to hand were an almost empty bag of corn chips and a cream cheese dip that had hardened, thankfully, before it could adhere to my fingers.

Maybe I was overreacting. The big man could simply be one of Artie's bowling buddies. "We're looking for Greg's mom, Donna," I said, intercepting him with my voice if not my body. "I guess she's with Artie."

"She didn't come home," Greg added.

The big man paused, at least the floor no longer vibrated with his movements. "She didn't come home. Geez that's tough." He sounded sincere.

During the pause that followed, you could almost hear the wheels turning in his head. "I should be pushing off. Check out some other places."

Only he didn't leave. He just stood there, uneasily shifting his weight from leg to leg. Maybe something about the two of us intrigued him. Or maybe, he somehow identified with Greg, had divorced parents, himself, or had lost one or the other of them in an accident.

"Do you know my Dad?" Greg persisted.

"Not exactly." So much for the bowling buddy hypothesis. I began to fear the worst again.

"Will you help us find him?" The way Greg said the words— boldness, shyness, hope all mixed in a single sentence, they came out half request and half prayer.

Again, I could sense those wheels turning. "I think I know one place he might be. Your Dad, I mean."

Something in Lionel's tone made me sure he was more certain than he sounded. And Greg's Dad was the only lead we had to Donna's disappearance. "Could we tag along?" I asked innocently.

"Sure," Lionel said. "I'd be happy to help the kid." Especially, the realization came to me, if you think he might get you in the door.

I decided to play coy with the big fellow. "I don't know, Greg," I began, dissembling. "Weren't there a few other places near here we should be looking for your mother first?"

"But if Lionel knows where my Dad is—"

"I think the kid wants to come." Lionel said. He was no longer being a nice guy.

"Maybe we will Lionel, " I replied, my tones as sweet as a zookeeper calming an 800-pound gorilla, "if you'd just cut out the bullshit and tell us why you want to find him." I smiled. Confrontation is often the quickest way to the truth. Of course, it's helpful if you keep an ice pack handy to cover the occasional bruise.

"You're awfully feisty for a blind guy." Lionel said.

"Try me."

"No thanks, you probably know Judo or something." His good-natured tone suggested he didn't give a shit one way or the other. "Kid, why don't you leave the room while I talk to your uncle."

Greg was not easily fooled; he wanted to be though. "It's something bad about my father, isn't it?"

"Not real bad."

"He owes you money, doesn't he?" Greg asked.

That would have been my first guess, well second, and I wasn't at all surprised when Lionel told me later, out of Greg's earshot, that he was an enforcer for a loan shark—"Artie's into my boss for a lot of money. We already know he didn't spend it on what he was supposed to."

What Lionel said to Greg then was that his father did owe money.

"A lot?" Greg asked.

We all knew what Greg wanted the answer to be. The big man thought for a moment. I could tell he wanted to say something nice, something reassuring, but there was nothing he could say.

Greg's footsteps clattered back up the hall.

"Hey, where you going kid?" Lionel asked.

"Just to get something."

Damn. I hoped Greg would have sense enough not to start a conversation with Girl while he was in the bedroom. I did and did not believe Lionel was being straight with us. Girl was the only edge we had.

To keep Lionel from following, I put my hand on his arm as if I needed assistance in walking and headed for the front door. It occurred to me as I did so that we were beginning to resemble a scene out of the Wizard of Oz: Greg as Dorothy, me as the scarecrow, and the cowardly Lionel (maybe). All we needed to complete the picture was a bimbo with a heart of gold or a tin man in search of one.

Chapter 5

Passers by might have thought it just another Sunday morning outing: Lionel in the driver's seat of his 1988 Cadillac with me, (his father? his older brother?) by his side; Greg, the grandson, in back, with the Frisbee and the deck of cards Greg had brought with him from his room. Hopefully, Girl was now trailing us several car lengths back.

She'd stayed hidden in Greg's bedroom the entire time Lionel was in the house. Our ace in the hole. I hadn't risked going back to talk with her for fear Lionel would overhear us. Her being behind us now in my Volvo was strictly blind faith on my part.

The guy parked next to us at the traffic light needed a valve job. Not my car then. Not that I was sure what my Volvo did sound like. From outside, I mean. How would I know when Girl was near?

Proof it was just another Sunday outing came when Greg announced he wanted to go to the bathroom. Lionel chuckled and pulled in at the first gas station we came to. He and I remained behind making forced conversation, with me trying to learn more from Lionel than he was willing to tell and Lionel doing likewise.

Lionel said he thought it was a shame, the poor kid's mother not coming home like that. I said it sure shot my plans for the day.

Lionel said she'd probably stayed over with the guy she'd been with the previous evening. I said she'd been with me most of the time, unless she'd had another blind date afterward.

Lionel's high-pitched giggle surprised both him and me.

"How'd you get that way, Professor? Blind I mean."

I guess he could tell I hadn't been born blind. "It was an explosion," I told him, the words coming easily for the first time, "at the Olympics. Someone set a bomb off in the park."

"Geez."

When Greg finally came back, his first words were, "Can I get a Coke?" Lionel gave him a buck and a half before I could get out my billfold, and we had Cokes all around.

Next stop was a drugstore. Lionel said he needed sunglasses, Greg said he needed them, too, and a Snickers bar. I nixed the Snickers bar—kids get much too much candy—"wait till afternoon at least," and the two of them looked at sunglasses while I waited by the front counter sniffing a display of men's cologne.

How far now to where Artie was staying? It seemed to me only a short time and a drive-through taco stand later when Greg and Lionel mutually decided we should stop at a grocery store to pick up the makings of lunch—apples and bananas for me, sandwiches from the deli for Lionel and Greg. I began to suspect we really weren't making progress toward our announced destination, nor did Lionel intend us to, we were simply wandering about aimlessly.

Had Lionel changed his mind about taking us to Greg's father?

I'd only the memory of too many turns to guide me. No point in asking Greg, his was the backseat view and indifference of the young. Half the time he hadn't been looking out the window but simply playing endlessly with the deck of Sorcery cards he'd brought with him. Girl could confirm my suspicions—if she were following us.

A second thought struck me. Had Lionel begun to suspect someone was tailing him? Were all these false turns and digressions simply to throw that someone off the scent? I would have to wait for Girl's appearance to be sure.

Chapter 6

I was standing by the apples, hefting a firm aromatic golden delicious, when I sensed her standing next to me. The pressure of her hand on my arm confirmed it. "You guys get around quite a bit," Girl said.

"But we don't actually seem to be getting anywhere."

She took a step back, to get a better view of me I supposed. "Boss, for a blind man you see a hell of a lot."

"Gas station, drug store, Del Taco, and now here. It's the long way round."

"Where are they now?"

"They're supposed to be off getting Twinkies." I pointed toward what I thought was the far corner of the store.

"Looks like they got a year's supply. Where did you get those walking shorts?" She chuckled and made a clicking sound with her tongue.

"Are they blue?"

"No. They're plaid. Bye Boss. Don't want them to catch me. " And she slipped off up the aisle.

Greg came up beside me. "Wasn't that Marci?" he whispered.

"Pick me up a few of these apples will you." I said in a loud voice. "Say nothing about seeing her," I hissed in a much lower one.

An ominous quiet followed or as quiet as it can get in a busy store on a late Sunday morning. Where had Greg gone? "Greg, did you hear me?"

"It's my Dad," I heard him say. Someone flew by me, I reached out, grabbed, let myself be tugged a few feet by Lionel. "Let go, professor." Then he, too, was gone.

The quiet of the 60-cycle fluorescent again, then someone standing near me waiting to take my place by the apples. I shuffled sideways and gave them the access they wanted. A woman, I thought, an oriental, though why I thought so, I don't know. Where was everybody?

"They're outside Boss, come with me." Girl's voice, then her hand leading me down the aisle and out the store. Hey, I wanted an apple.

"Who's here?" I demanded of no one and everyone once we were outside.

"Greg and Lionel."

"Greg's Dad?"

"Got away, professor," Lionel said, then added, "Who's the girl?"

"A friend," I began.

"Marci works for the professor," Greg finished.

"Has she been following us?" Lionel's deep boom demanded.

"Lionel," I began calmly, taking a step in the direction of his voice. I sensed Girl was stepping forward with me, caught the movement of her silhouette out of the corner of my eye.

"Yes, Professor." He let me take his arm; a big mistake, I knew Girl was moving up on his other side.

"Lionel, you've been jerking us around, a stop for a piss here, a stop for sun glasses at another place. I thought you were taking us to where Greg's Dad was staying."

"Greg's the one who wanted to stop at those places," he mumbled and tried to step back; but I stepped right back with him, bringing up an ice pick from my jacket just as Girl swept the legs out from beneath him. He fell heavily; the big ones always do.

I slid forward alongside and down beside him, one knee bent, my ice pick right behind his ear. "Don't get up," I said and made sure he knew the ice pick was there.

Greg gasped. Girl said to someone off to the side, "Our friend slipped, he'll be okay in a moment."

"Where are you taking us?" I hissed into Lionel's ear.

"I'll take you, I promise. I just didn't want—"

"Too late for promises, big guy. And I didn't ask when, I asked where. Give me the address."

"But—"

Too late for "buts, too. Lionel gave me the address and I had Girl write it down. It was time once again to take command.

Chapter 7

Once the address of Artie's hideout was out in the open, Lionel was calmer. It seemed he'd felt trapped between what he thought he should do and what he thought his boss would want him to do. "You see Professor, I wasn't sure exactly he would want you to know about Artie's hiding places.

"But a kid ought to know where his father is, ain't that right?"

The sweat had evaporated from his large body by then, but a slight residual tang of fear remained. I agreed that it was right, grateful Lionel bore no animosity and that the gentle giant was, for the moment, back on our side. But I kept my ice pick handy just in case.

We all piled into Lionel's car, me beside Lionel in the front seat, Greg traveling with Marci in the back. Turns out we weren't that far from Artie's hideout, which is why Lionel had spotted him buying cigarettes at the grocery check stand.

I had Lionel drive past the house where Artie was supposed to be staying and in and out of a cul de sac before I felt confident of the approach. A block away, I assembled my troops. "Greg and I will go in together. Lionel, you and Girl cut off the escape routes; Greg's Dad may just decide to make it out through a window."

"Give us five minutes," Girl said, which gave Greg and I a chance to do a little more of the buddy-buddy bit. Turns out he liked health science, my favorite, was having some trouble with math, who doesn't, and wasn't sure about his compositional skills, work on it. We were side by side with Greg's hand on my arm when we rang the bell.

The man and the woman who came to the door together were surprisingly young. They smelled of Patchouli oil, an aroma I thought had gone out with the sixties. I wondered if he had a scraggly beard and if she were thin and braless, with long black hair streaming down her back.

The young man stuttered. After his initial, "Can we help you?" he let his wife do most of the talking. She carried a baby, who shifted restlessly throughout the conversation. From it's not too faint smell of urine, I could readily imagine why.

In response to our, "We're looking for Greg's Dad," a third voice, an older woman's, joined in from the back of the room. The grandmother or grandmother-in-law said quickly, too quickly, "He doesn't live here."

"But he's been staying with you." I persisted.

"No," from the grandmother, "ye..ye..yess," from the stutterer, and "he left, we don't know whether he'll be back," from the girl.

"Hey," the young man said in response to the step I'd taken through their doorway.

"Greg would like to see his Dad."

"Yes, but you just can't walk in here like that."

"Oh my God, someone's in the back yard." This last from the grandmother.

People began moving about me, all talking at once, no one listening to anyone else, like characters in a Chekhov play. I had trouble keeping track of who was where, except for the brief intervals in which each one said his or her lines. The prowler in the garden, was it Girl? Lionel? A total stranger?

"Oh my God," the girl said. The prowler had to be Lionel; Girl would never have inspired a fraction of that fear.

"The weasel got away again," Lionel howled, stepping in through the sliding glass window.

"Who are you?" the mother-in-law demanded.

"Look, he's bleeding." said the girl.

"You just can't come into our house like that."

I called for quiet and got it from all but the mother-in-law, who continued muttering in the background, and the baby, who cried and had to be comforted by his mother. We searched the home, leaving Lionel to stand guard in the living room, and found that yes, indeed, Artie had been living with them. I took Lionel into the bathroom then and, after washing my own hands and arms twice like a surgeon, poured cold water over the thin trickle of blood that could be felt against his massive biceps.

"He had a knife this time," Lionel said.

I soaped Lionel's arm, since he seemed afraid to do it himself, then rinsed it a second time. Didn't even need a Band-Aid. He was the cowardly lionel, all right.

We stayed in the house just long enough for the grandmother-in-law to get in another rejoinder and then reassembled back out on the sidewalk. "Let's explore the neighborhood," I said as we waved goodbye to the happy family. I didn't imagine Artie would be a welcome guest in their home again, but you never can tell about people.

The area, several miles inland, had a mixture of forest and desert smells, and the ever-present aroma of suburbia, dry-bark mulch, wet green lawns, sprinklers. We hadn't gone more than a block on foot when Greg exclaimed, "That's Dad's car."

"So," Lionel began and the growl he emitted would have frightened any grizzly.

I held up my hand, "I'll handle it."

I could hear the growl and then a grunt as Girl intercepted the advancing Lionel. "He'll handle it," she said.

I knocked on the car window. Rustling sounds suggested a man trying to bury himself deep in the seat cushions. I knocked again and intakes of breath from behind me announced a man's face had appeared in the window.

"Greg." I beckoned with my fingers and Greg came forward. The car door opened and Greg slipped inside. A moment later and he and his Dad stepped out together.

"I understand you're on my side," Artie said. I shook my head. "I mean you're not going to let Lionel beat me up or nothing." I made an equivocal gesture with my hand. "See, I've been looking for Greg's mom, too. I guess I should have phoned the boy, told him where I was."

"Thinks fast on his feet," I heard Girl say behind me echoing what I was thinking.

"Tell us where she is, Artie."

"I don't know or I would tell you. I mean, we don't live together or nothing." He sounded sincere, but I sensed he'd had a lot of practice sounding that way.

"Let's go back to your friends' place."

"They don't want any trouble." he said, expressing a concern for others I would hardly have expected from him. Perhaps his extended visit was not an entirely welcome one.

"Just want a cup of tea Artie. Maybe Girl and Lionel want something. I know Greg wants a glass of milk."

"I'd like a coke," Greg said with adolescent enthusiasm.

"Milk."

Artie interrupted our discussion. "You're not going to let him get me?"

"You're safe while we're with you." An ambiguous promise, but one I'm sure Artie recognized was the best he was going to get under the circumstances.

Halfway to the hideout, he began sidling away to a different drummer, but a growl from Lionel soon returned him to our little group.

"Take my arm, please," I suggested tactfully. "I'll need help getting on and off the curb."

"I'd rather take the bimbo's," Artie replied, but a plaintive "Dad!" from Greg and a shove from Lionel brought him safely to my side.

Artie's friends were not anxious to see us. They knew better than to argue with Lionel, though, and decided it was the appropriate time to take the baby for a walk in the stroller. Their decision was not unanimous for they began yelling at each other the instant they stepped out the door. I heard the girl screaming, "I want him out of here." The boy mumbled something in reply. "You can't speak to my daughter like that," from the grandmother was followed immediately by a waking cry from the baby, and then, thankfully, they moved out of earshot.

Again Artie showed an inclination to leave our party, following after his friends, but Girl and Lionel manhandled him into the kitchen.

"Where's Donna?" I asked in a conversational tone once we were all seated together at the kitchen table, tea cups and glasses in hand. (No, Greg did not get a coke.)

"How should I know?"

"She's your wife."

"Shit, we been separated four years."

"Watch your language." This last admonition came from Lionel.

"Why didn't you pick up your boy earlier?" I asked.

"I was going to this evening. Donna had a date and asked me to help out."

No use asking why Artie hadn't wanted to spend the whole day with his child. He obviously had his own priorities.

"Shall I check the bedroom boss?" Girl asked.

"Do it."

Artie made a motion to get up from the table, and I waved him down.

For a few moments the only sounds were a ticking wall clock and a faucet that called for immediate repair.

"No signs of Greg's mom," Girl reported as soon as she rejoined us. "Do you think we should check the hospitals?"

"We'll do that next." (Mentally, I kicked myself for not doing it first thing that morning.)

"You want to stay with your father or go with us?" I asked Greg.

"Stay with you."

I got up then and signaled for Girl and Greg to follow me. "We'll wait for you in the car Lionel." Artie's cry of anguish was music to my ears.

## Chapter 8

"We're not going to find my mom," Greg said when we'd returned to my apartment. His voice, empty and lifeless, echoed my own lack of satisfaction.

Sure we are," I said, though I wasn't sure of anything. "Now, we found your Dad, right?"

Greg didn't reply. Apparently he'd found the two meetings with his Dad cold comfort. He tried amusing himself by dealing out his sorcery cards on the couch in my living room, but his pain was too immediate to be held in check for long by fantasy. "And we've got Lionel working for us." I noted. This got me a grunt, though it might have been a whimper. Whatever, it caused Greg to sink even deeper into the big overstuffed armchair I keep for company.

Our calls to hospitals near Donna's house and In Cahoots had been unsuccessful. Which was good news the way I figured it. I dispatched Girl to Greg's house to talk with their neighbors, but I didn't have much hope for that either. Tomorrow morning, we would call the police.

"Okay, so where does your mother go?" I asked, "Who are her friends?" A dumb question, about as smart as asking Greg for driving instructions to his home. Kids don't drive, and they don't know who their parent's friends are. "Who was she dating?" I asked.

"No one," he said, "you, I guess; you said you had a date."

"Frank?" The name had come back to me suddenly. The three figures in the darkened racetrack, the smell of eucalyptus, horse dung, and two men and a woman, the woman struggling to get free.

"No, he's just someone my mother met at my dance lesson. I think he knows my father though."

Damn. I began to regret giving Lionel his time alone with Artie. I realized now, too late, a lot more questions remained for Artie Clark to answer. I just hoped he was still able to talk.

"Who was supposed to take you to your dance lesson?" I asked.

Before Greg could reply, Girl's cheerful voice announced "Dinner" from the front hallway.

"I was going to fix us all something." I said.

"Sure you were," Marci retorted. "Peanut butter sandwiches and apples, same as breakfast." She turned and spoke to Greg, "I brought us good food from the Colonel."

Greg may have been less disconsolate at the thought of food; I couldn't see his expression. "I don't eat that garbage," I said.

Girl ignored my ill humor. "I brought you a salad, Boss, and I'll fix you a baked potato in the microwave."

"I'd like a potato," Greg said. He was feeling better, then. At least for the moment. Now, if I could only live up to his renewed expectations.

Girl used the opportunity provided by our meal to ask Greg more or less the same questions I'd already asked him. "Who else does your mother spend time with?"

"Dates and things?"

"No. Just people, neighbors, stuff like that."

"The Reverend," Greg said. He had quieted suddenly.

"Who's that?"

"You know, he's the preacher at the church we go to." The words came slowly from Greg's mouth. He twisted in his chair and rubbed his arms as he spoke.

Girl's voice was gentle in reply. "Greg. You're not telling us something. What was your mother talking to the Reverend about?"

The longish pause seemed to stretch to eternity. Greg picked at his skin, and I felt like shouting, "Stop." Fortunately,

35

the interval was much longer for Greg than it was for Marci and I.

"She was talking to him about me," Greg admitted, "See, I don't have a Dad or anything, not really..."

Girl waited for him to complete the unfinished sentence, but all we heard for several moments was Greg's uneven breathing, his hands tearing at his face, a mumbling sound as if he were talking to himself.

"You got in some kind of trouble," Girl filled in for him.

A mumbled, "Yes" in reply. Greg was again on the verge of tears.

"At school?" I could tell Girl was just guessing, but Greg responded as if he were truly pleased someone understood.

"I was getting in fights."

"I got in a lot of fights when I was in school," I interjected before Girl shushed me. Who was the boss here anyway?

"Guys made fun about my dancing. My Dad said I should never back down."

Funny thing for a guy who hid in the back seats of cars to say.

"And the Reverend?"

"He just said I should pray. And he wanted to know if I took cold showers."

I couldn't help myself; I laughed out loud.

"Boss," Marci chided.

Time for me to speak up, take command. "We'll go see the Reverend this evening after we've put the dishes away. And then we'll take you to your dance lesson.

"Now, eat! This stuff will never last the night in my refrigerator."

Chapter 9

Before going anywhere, I wanted to hear Girl's report on her visit to Greg and Donna's neighborhood. Chewing noises intercepted many of her words. Girl has a healthy appetite—I don't always approve of what she eats—and once the bucket from the Colonel was eliminated, she set about raiding my refrigerator looking for nutritional supplements.

"It's sort of like our neighborhood, boss, maybe a little more upscale. All houses, small ones, no apartments."

I thought of rising to the defense of my own eight-unit garden complex, but decided to let it go.

"The two neighbors on either side are pretty much see-no-evil, hear-no-evil. One family is Vietnamese. The grandmother and grandfather don't speak English. But their grandchild, who's a couple of years older than Greg—"

"Two years older," Greg put in.

"—speaks pure American. Her parents, she says, are either working or sleeping. She didn't hear anything last night, only she went to bed early. She's studying for exams. Says she wants to go to Berkeley."

"I got all my degrees at Berkeley. It's a miserable place."

"Well, that's what she wants. She says Greg's a sweet boy and Donna is a very nice person."

"Visitors?" I questioned.

"As I said, she doesn't see, doesn't hear anything except what's happening immediately around her. Keep in mind, she's 17, trying to pass exams and have a good time with her friends."

"All her friends are Oriental," Greg said.

"The other house?" I prompted before we could get bogged down in ethnicities.

"They belong to Donna's church, too. We may meet them again this afternoon. He's older, doesn't have all his teeth. She's older, but pretends to be younger. They're the sort that would see and report everything, but they're always off on church business, according to them. They've also got some sort of store."

"He complains about me to mom a lot," said Greg.

"Yeah, they really had it in for you, tall guy. But they thought Donna was okay if she'd just go back to her husband."

"Mr. Gaddis is always telling her that."

"I had the impression Mrs. Gaddis was a little more accepting, but I could have been wrong."

"And last night?" I made a hand motion for Girl to get to the point.

"Didn't see anything, didn't hear anything, went to bed early. No midnight noises or rows to disturb them. Says Donna seldom has visitors, although Greg has noisy friends."

"Just the guys from school."

I was glad to hear about the friends. I didn't want to think Greg spent all his time dancing with his mom.

"Oh and the Reverend calls on her. Just last week at that."

"Nobody told me," Greg began, but Girl shushed him.

"Across the street, the guy tried to put the moves on me; he's about six feet three, built like a horse, and almost as hairy; but then his wife came to the door. Totally hostile. Claimed she didn't even know the names of the people who lived across the way. Wouldn't let me ask her husband the same question.

"One door up was the real find, Mrs. Clara Hansen, or Mrs. Walter Hansen as she first introduced herself, though I gather Walter is long gone to the big place in the sky. Doesn't get out much anymore except when someone is kind enough to take her to church, and doesn't get much sleep—suffers from insomnia she claims, which means she's on guard duty 24 hours a day."

A smile lit up my face. We'd have some real leads, finally.

"Greg is a noisy boy but so are all the kids in the neighborhood, little beasts most of them. Greg is okay, at least when his mother is around, but watch out when she takes off."

An immediate objection from Greg was cut short by my finger an inch from his face.

"Donna has good manners," Girl continued. "So does Greg, again, when his mother is around. It's the lady next door that concerns her, the pit bull that almost bit me for ogling her husband."

"You were ogling her husband? All that hair, was that what did it?"

"In his dreams. It seems they have a son about Greg's age."

"Billy," Greg said.

"Greg, let her tell the story."

"And Billy has an older friend, a 12th grader who walks him home sometimes. Greg, maybe you'd better go in the other room."

Greg started to get up, but I put out a restraining arm. He moved closer to me on the couch. We were two buddies, partners against a world of hostile females.

"You both settled? I can tell my story?" Girl didn't wait for an answer. "Well, one afternoon, the friend shows up early before school is out. The next afternoon he shows up after school, but Billy doesn't get home until much later."

"Soccer practice."

"You can guess the rest."

Fascinating as was this introduction to Westminster's own Peyton Place, I determined to steer the conversation back to my own parochial interests. "What about Donna?" I asked, emphasizing each word with outstretched fingers.

"She left about 7 p.m., leaving Greg alone in the house watching television. He fell asleep about nine, but didn't actually go to bed until eleven. She did not come home, nor did any car park anywhere nearby after ten.

"Donna had two visitors the previous week: the Reverend, and a second man who came by twice, one time when Donna was at home and once when she wasn't. Mrs. Hansen thinks it might have been Donna's ex-husband."

We couldn't have done better with surveillance cameras. "Thanks, kid." I stretched, arms extended, wondering as always how far my fingertips were from the ceiling. My backbone eased gratefully into place, though my butt was still sore from too much couch time. My muscles craved action. So did I. "Let's go see the Reverend."

Chapter 10

But another problem need be dealt with first. "Don't you have an appointment with Miss Woo?"

Miss Woo was right up with the frogs, locusts, and other plagues, though maybe a step below having one's firstborn done away with. I'll admit I never would have been able to live as independently after the explosion as I do today without the help of innumerable government agencies. But having to deal with an endless series of self-righteous officials has turned me into a Libertarian, convinced government should never, ever be permitted to interfere in the affairs of the individual.

Miss Woo, my vocational counselor, was the prototypical bureaucrat. She knew what was best for me and had little or no intention of listening to evidence to the contrary. Remarkably old for one so young—Marci put Woo at somewhere between twenty-four and twenty-eight years of age—her thinking was set in rigid lines and her hearing, in so far as it concerned the opinions of others, virtually nonexistent.

Her saving graces were mainly hidden from me. She was attractive, so Marci said, with a pretty face even by Western standards and an almost boyish figure (not much as far as bust and hips went), graceful, and lively. This last, at least, was not lost on me. If only Woo would listen!

"You should be a teacher."

"I was a University professor for sixteen years."

"High school, perhaps."

"I taught Anatomy at the Pacific College of Osteopathy for the last six. I was the chairman of the department."

"English, perhaps, I think you would be very good at English literature, you read so much."

I listened to books on tape if that is what she meant, and I still had a library, mainly Ross MacDonald, Bernard Malamud, Dick Frances, and whatever my ex-wife left behind from the book club she once belonged to. But English? Give it a rest, Woo. As for high school, forget it.

No one listens in high school; even the students who do care, the few that still exist, do all their studying at home. Too much socializing going on, too much concern with what others (not the teacher) are saying and doing.

To get the students attention away from their hormones for even a fraction of time, I would have to become some sort of entertainer. Worse, I would have to treat them as individuals, to care whether they learned anything I taught.

The first year medical students whom I instructed at Pacific, the ones who survived, had mastered one important concept: pass anatomy or take up a new career. Professor Anders could be mean, sarcastic, impatient. They knew they'd have to do the work I assigned or sell retail for a living.

I taught in a community college once: a dreadful experience, students concerned with how little they need learn to pass, students who protested every lost point, who wanted make-up exams. No, teaching in a high school or a two-year college was out.

Besides, in high school, students were the least of the instructor's worries. Managerial drones and indulgent parents exist only to make life for the professional still more miserable.

"Maybe I could be a crossing guard?"

"That is a silly idea; you can't see. Oh, you are making joke." (Ah hah, she did listen.) "We haven't time for jokes; we must find you a career."

And so we would go once again through her sad little list of improbable occupations. Did it never occur to her that I was happy with my roses and my books-on-tape, that the occasional evening spent dancing and the occasional partner who came afterward to bed were enough for me?

"You are young." (I was twice her age.) "You are an educated man, you need to have a career. And you must never give up."

Here she would tell me some dreadful story about a person who had given way to despondency, lain all day in bed (so I had greeted Miss Woo once or twice while wearing a bathrobe) but now led a happy productive life working in the back of a florists arranging bouquets.

Actually, I think I would enjoy working in a florist's. I love flowers and give my friends roses from my garden at every opportunity. But the florist, according to Miss Woo, was not for me. I was an educated man. I would teach high school English.

"She likes you," Marci said.

"I'm a challenge."

"She's only required to make one visit, perhaps two, but here she's come to see you a half dozen weeks in row."

"Well, tell her I'm not here this evening. I've got things to do. We've got things to do."

"You'll want to see her today."

"Big deal."

"She's wearing her off-duty clothes: form-fitting black toreadors, a sleeveless white top, and a soft bra."

"How can you tell about the bra?"

"Headlights."

I was glad Greg was out of the way while Marci and I had this conversation. Or was he? "Where's Greg?"

"Watching T.V."

I met your son; he a fine boy," Miss Woo called out, ebullient as ever, as she bounced into the room. "Handsome like father."

I thought of correcting her, telling her I only had daughters so far, but the thought never became words. What if Greg were to be my boy? Some time in the future I mean, after we'd got his mother back. I'd be proud to have him as a son.

"He remind me of my brother back in Taiwan. He be going to college soon, of course. All the reason to think about your own career. Have you given more thought to teaching high school? I brought some brochures; we can read them together."

We read them, at least she did, and when she was gone the smell of apple blossoms and litchi nuts lingered in the room.

Chapter 11

Reverend Boyle was just about the meanest man I ever met,
mean as in mean-spirited, sanctimonious, petty, money-
grubbing and any other Dickensonian epithet you'd like to
apply. He also was short and ugly, but I had to have Girl point
this out to me.

What masochistic urge would drive someone to become a
member of this sorry-excuse for a petty-thief's flock?

Tracking him down hadn't been easy. First, we had Greg's
ill-defined directions to cope with. He led us with some
difficulty to what he said was the church, but the minister
that greeted us at the rectory door was a grinning Korean. We
soon learned the church was a shared building with
Vietnamese Methodists, New Christians (the Reverend's
group), and Korean Presbyterians all taking their turns in the
chapel. Late Sunday afternoon, the Reverend was to be found
around the back and down the stairs in the basement.

A good-sized flock awaited us; apparently the New
Christians took their church seriously, with services extending
throughout the day. We were welcomed by too many people
with insincere handshakes, then told to be quiet until the
Reverend was through.

The Reverend was against Catholics, Muslims, established
Protestant religions, sex (in or out of wedlock), nudism (hard
to envision this as a particularly pressing issue), gambling, sex
(a topic the Reverend returned to frequently), abortion (a
woman ought to be punished for having sex by having to bear
the product of her sin), divorce (ditto), cigarettes, liquor,
movies, books, dancing, and anything else that might keep a
family from tithing. He professed a great love for the Jewish
people while decrying their stubborn refusal to recognize the

true savior. He warned young men against idleness and self-abuse; he warned young women against temptation. He praised the sacrament of Christian marriage and denounced its dissolution. Which made it a bit tough on Donna and any other single mothers in the audience. I gathered the status of a divorced woman within the New Christians was about on the order of Mary Magdalene or the woman taken in adultery.

The Reverend remained seated throughout most of these exhortations, making his points by tapping his fingers on a large book held out before him—a bible, presumably. He also clacked his teeth together at odd moments, a habit I found off-putting.

Sermon over (the third of the day for the Good Reverend) we experienced another round of handshakes, while all around us parishioners exchanged hugs, with some, mainly men, taking it upon themselves to hug Girl.

The Reverend shook my hand and told me how much Jesus loved the blind. He asked me if I'd care to drop to my knees and pray. I said that I would, I surely would, but that a deeper, more pressing, more Godly mission had brought me to his home that day. ("You are such a ham," Girl said later.)

When he pressed me for details, I asked Greg to step forward. The subsequent reaction to Greg's presence is what set me against that church forever. In their impious minds, Greg was, and would always be, that awful boy. Yes, Christ did forgive those that had sinned, though they may have sinned a hundred times, but first, it appeared, that sinner must have true repentance in his heart. Since Greg had little or no idea what those sins might be, and as they probably consisted at most of the occasional masturbatory fantasy, I wondered where the Reverend thought he was getting off assigning guilt and blame. I would have told him what I felt but for Girl's restraining hand on my arm.

"We're looking for Donna, Greg's mother; we hoped she might have come here today." Girl said sweetly. From the buzz of conversation that rose around us, I gathered Donna no longer came to church, having failed somehow to live up to her reputation as a fallen woman.

"We can only hope she is with her husband," the Reverend intoned unctuously, which shows how little the Reverend knew about that scumbag, and/or how little he cared.

"Thank you," I said, closing off the conversation, and used my blindness, stumbling deliberately, to clear a path for all of us from the room. The many cries to "come back, we'd like to have you with us next Sunday," only made me want to walk away faster.

Once we were out in the parking lot, where warmth and sunlight, God's sunlight, was again all about us, Greg pulled on my arm, dragging me aside. I gathered he didn't want Girl to hear us.

"Do you think the Reverend was right," Greg asked me, "that maybe I ought to try ..."

"No. No! No." I was shouting and forced myself to deliberately lower my voice. "You're okay, I'm okay We both have God within us."

"But," Greg began.

"No buts." I would have to have long talks with this boy whom more and more I was treating as my son.

Girl walked up to us then, and sang in my ear in a deliberately high-pitched falsetto, "Someone wants to talk to you."

I swiveled my head wondering whom she was talking about.

Still using that singsong voice, Girl said, "I don't know who she is, but she's tall, fills out her sweater beautifully, and has murder in her eye."

A hint of gardenias preceded the newcomer; an older woman's perfume, perhaps, but she had a young woman's voice, a warm caressing alto—she could sing in my choir any day. "I want to talk to you," she began and I sensed that Girl and Greg, those cowards, had stepped back out of the way.

"I've seen you dancing with Donna. You know she is a married woman—"

"You must be the sister-in-law." I intuited.

"No. I'm just a friend, a friend of hers and her good husband Arthur. I don't want to see their marriage broken up, a Christian marriage."

"Thank you for warning me," I said politely, wondering what else I could say to encourage her to go away.

"I wasn't thinking of you."

"Of course you were. Warning me was the Christian thing to do. An entanglement with a married woman could only hurt me in the end."

"Donna and Arthur are my friends," she began a second time. "What you are doing is wrong."

I cast about for any sins I might have committed, again apart from masturbatory fantasies. I'd danced with Donna, rescued her from two apes holding her against her will, spent the best part of a day paling around with her son, and saved her ex-husband from a dreadful beating. Nope, I didn't feel guilty.

Aloud, I said facetiously, "I'm puzzled; you don't have the least concern that I might get hurt in the relationship. I have feelings, too, you know, and if Donna's still not divorced, you should have warned me."

"As a Christian, I was just concerned about my friend and her husband."

"As a Christian?" My voice was louder now. No one in the back row of a 1200-seat teaching amphitheater would have had the slightest difficulty hearing me. "I am a Christian." I boomed, "Don't you dare use that word on me as if it were some kind of experience unique to you alone. That of God is in each of us. If you really want to help Donna, you'll make sure she never has to see her scumbag ex-husband again."

I heard the sound of clicking heels and a rustling skirt moving away from me across the pavement, and behind me, where Girl and Greg were standing, a faint round of applause from long girlish fingers.

Chapter 12

I hate going to new places, I mean places I hadn't gone to
before I lost my eyesight. Somebody has to walk me to the
front door. I have to go slow in case the building has steps to
surmount and if so I need to learn how many steps there are
and how high each one is. I even have to bring my cane.

The trip to the dance studio was still more complicated.
Because our objective was to trap Frank, I couldn't just go in
and out the front door, but had to tour the entire facility to
learn where the back entrances were. Mirrors and doorways
popped up in unexpected locations; each time I had to be kept
from walking into them. A wooden handrail designed to assist
the dancers stuck out from the far wall of the large main room
and was another watch-it.

"He's here," Greg said, almost the minute we walked in the
door.

"Frank? Is his friend here, too?" I sensed the answer was
"no" well before Greg replied.

"Are you going to go get him?"

I patted Greg on the shoulder. "Not just yet. We've got to
figure out a way to lure him outside first."

Greg's excitement ebbed quickly and he began to shift
restlessly from foot to foot. I wasn't too stimulated myself; I
craved action. It would come soon enough, I knew.

"How many people are here?" I asked Marci.

"Twenty-five. Thirty."

Greg changed positions once too often and almost knocked
over a mirror. "Sorry. Do you think I should take the dance
lesson?"

Girl answered for us, "Yes Greg, I think you should."

The boy ran off eagerly, glad to be doing something he was good at, something over which he had some control.

"Do you think we ought to take the lessons?" Girl asked, "I'm beginning to think we stand out like a sore thumb."

I wasn't sure we could. Usually they charged. And you had to sign up for an entire series. Girl was right though; we had to stay inconspicuous until we decided what we were going to do.

"Okay, you'll start out as my partner. I'll try to teach you how to fake it."

"Boss, I can get it."

"West Coast Swing is very difficult. It can take years to learn."

"Boss, how do you think I got my brown belt?"

We took our place with the others; I could only hope Girl had sense enough to imitate the women on either side of her. The instructor took us quickly through his standard warm-up with Girl fighting just to retain her balance.

"Now, comes the easiest part of class," I told her.

Girl pressed my hand; she didn't yet have a clue what I was talking about.

The instructor's gravelly two-pitched voice, a bass line with a throaty treble riding on top of it, spoke out. "Now comes the easiest part of class. Men, say goodbye to your partners. Ladies, I want you to each move one partner to the left."

"What'll I do?" Girl said.

"Fake it." I took the new woman's hand. Sea air and honey. Brigitte. "I didn't expect to see you so soon," she said. "From the way you behaved on Saturday, I thought you had a new steady girl friend."

"I'm here with her kid."

"Greg? Isn't he a good dancer? And he's only 13." She giggled and cuddled against me. "You're not supposed to be here you know.

"Don't worry," she added as I started to draw away, "I told the instructor you were a wizard on the dance floor."

I disengaged myself and pointed to my chest, "That's me, the Wizard of Oz."

"Oh, no, you're the exact opposite of him."

I shook my head, puzzled.

"Oz was a wonderful man and a terrible Wizard."

The lesson was a good one, fast-paced, with some interesting new syncopations. I sort of wished I'd signed up for the course. The instructor had us change partners frequently, so I was not burdened with Brigitte for long. On the down side, not all my partners were as skillful, and some were patronizing. "Nuit de Paris" yielded to "Passion" and then to apple blossoms.

"Miss Woo?" I cried as a firm hand grasped mine.

"Shh. We must listen to the teacher."

Thirty seconds and already she was telling me what to do. "I didn't know you took lessons."

"Today, first day. Please, quiet; we need listen."

Things got worse. "You're not doing what the instructor say," Woo told me.

"I did a variation."

"I don't know about variation. And you must move your feet to the beat and take my hand, so."

This could not be happening. Six years of lessons on my part, one day on hers, and this Red Army apparatchik was telling me what to do!

Thankfully, Woo's apple blossoms yielded to "Chansons des fleurs" and then to gardenias.

Gardenias? I sniffed aloud, checking to be sure. "Is it my little friend from the parking lot?" I questioned. My new partner stammered something inaudible, still I recognized her alto voice. We stood awkwardly in the ready position, her right hand in my left, both of us praying, I'm sure, for the instructor to get on with it. But no, he had chosen that moment to give personal instruction to Brigitte.

"You're a good dancer," my Christian friend said, along with "Thank you," before we parted company.

I heard the shouting long before the dance teacher and the others had decided it was an unwelcome disturbance. Girl and someone else—was it Frank?—arguing in the doorway. Girl screaming like an outraged prostitute whose client had tried to stiff her. "You put your hand on my tit." A slap. Frank tried to retaliate, for the next voice was that of a strange male saying, "Keep your hands off her."

Retrieving my cane from the wall where I'd left it, I made my way through the press, using my cane and my elbows to good advantage. Even the outraged backed off. I was right behind Frank when, sensibly, he realized retreat was the better part of valor and headed for the exit door. Just as he crossed the threshold, my cane entangled in his thrashing feet and he went down with a thump on the pavement. Before he could complete the natural string of obscenities, I was on him. Behind my back, hopefully, Girl was blocking the progress of other would-be vigilantes.

"Where is Donna?" I asked, my cane planted firmly across Frank's throat.

"I don't know."

"You want to tell me."

A strangled moan said he did want to.

"You danced with her yesterday."

"I won't dance with her again," he gasped.

Though I'd just as soon have discouraged all of Donna's potential dancing partners, I feared Frank had misunderstood my motives. "Tell me *why* you wanted to talk with her." I brought the cane up from his throat and against his chin so he could breathe.

"I'm a friend of Artie's." he said. I looked bored.

"Artie and I had a business deal." I looked interested.

"I find things. I bring people with common interests together. Say something will you?"

I replied with a grunt.

Frank's words grew faster, closer together. "I introduced Artie to some people who sell things, n' then I brought him together with some other guys who arrange financing."

What was I, an economist? "Pretend I'm dumb, Frank. Spell it out, detail by detail. Draw me a diagram if you have to."

Frank took a deep breath, choked momentarily on his own saliva and then began again. "Artie wanted to buy crack, large quantities. How he planned to sell it, I don't know, probably had a couple of other guys he was going to wholesale to. He needed money to finance the deal. I introduced him to Massoud Favor. He pays Massoud 20% of what he borrows in interest each week. Who cares, it's a cost of doing business."

"Lionel?"

"The big guy? Yeah, he works for Massoud. See, I get five percent. Five percent of the loan, five percent of what the people sell.

"I haven't got paid yet and I don't care. I just want to get out from under. See Artie didn't deliver. He didn't deliver the dope, he didn't deliver the money."

I could see Frank had big problems. If they couldn't squeeze Artie, Frank was the next logical choice. "Who sold Artie the dope?"

"You don't want to know."

I stuck my finger up Frank's nose.

"Jesus," he said, when his coughing fit stopped. "Just ask me when you want to know something. They're Colombians, they all live together. Five or six of them. An Alvarao, a Carlos, and a Raoul, the usual. I can hardly tell them apart."

"Take me to them."

"Now?"

What part of "now" didn't Frank understand? I eased him to his feet, my cane under his chin, and walked him to his car.

"I've always wanted to visit Santa Ana." I said, visualizing the tough Mexican barrio we were headed for.

"Santa Ana?" Frank sounded incredulous, "You don't understand drugs do you? We're going to Newport Beach."

## Chapter 13

This time Girl made no secret of the fact she was right behind me. At least, I hoped that was her taking off in my Volvo.

Frank's car was a smog generator and it struck me he couldn't be all that much of a success in his chosen procession. His choice of radio programs sucked and after despairing of his presets, I just hit the scanner till I found something I wanted to listen to.

"What's the matter with Country?" he wanted to know.

"Nothing, as long as it's on the dance floor." Give me jazz or classical if I'm not going to dance. Give me a woodwind quintet if you want to see me in heaven.

The air grew cooler quickly as we approached the beach and the tang of salt air and kelp cut through the stench of freeway gasoline.

"Where are we now?" I asked Frank.

"On MacArthur, about a block from PCH. The Colombians live in an apartment house on Avocado."

"Mirror and white walls in the lobby?"

"Yeah. You weren't always blind, uh."

I shook my head.

"That explains why you got such good taste in women. I mean like Donna's not a 10 or anything, but she's not a bimbo."

Another grunt from me.

"You going to go in?" he asked as we slowed in front of the building.

I shook my head a second time. "Cruise down the street, where we can see who is going in and out. We'll wait for my friends."

It didn't take long before Girl's head appeared at my window. "We're here Boss. Looks like we're just in time for the party."

Frank spoke up, "That's Carlos standing in front of the building. The one with the glass in his hand."

I pushed open the car door, Girl helping me, and stepped out on the curb. "Get lost," I said, giving the car roof a slap. Frank got.

"Tell me again where we are."

Girl described the setting. "And how you're dressed." The clothes she'd worn to dance class would certainly enable her to bewitch any male.

"Greg and I will go for a walk." I told Girl. "It's your party."

Girl touched my lips with her fingertips and walked off hips swinging.

"What's she doing?" I asked Greg. We stood quietly where Girl had left us.

"Just walking. She's almost in front of the building. The guy standing in front of it called out to her. Now, she's talking to him."

"Putting the moves on."

"I guess." Greg seemed embarrassed.

"And now?"

"They're still just talking."

"Let's go for our walk, maybe we can see the ocean."

When we returned from our walk—we'd smelled the ocean, a line of tall houses kept us from a view–Girl had disappeared. Inside the apartment house? Probably. Too much time passed while we waited for her to return. "Let's sit in the car." Greg and I sat, listened to the radio. Girl could be gone all night.

A smart guy like me should have anticipated this. "How are we going to get out of here?"

"I'll drive," Greg's boy-man voice volunteered.

The idea of Greg driving was absurd, and it took almost another hour of waiting, well, forty-five minutes, before it began to sound like a plan.

Chapter 14

We were rescued, sort of. My rescuer was 13 years old and didn't have a driver's permit. Still he seemed to be doing okay so far. The bumps bothered me. He appeared to be lining up the car on the median to steer and whenever we hit the warning markers, the shock communicated itself to my fillings.

Take-off had been delayed while Greg fiddled with mirrors and seat backs, but the rapidity of our launch more than made up for it. My first indication that something was really wrong came when Greg said, "The car behind us is flashing its lights, what should I do?"

Naturally, I asked what color the lights were, although I already suspected what Greg's answer would be. We pulled over to the curb before the police officer could turn on the siren.

"Where are we?" I asked Greg out of the corner of my mouth.

"That big street that comes out of the highway." Kids these days; you're lucky if they know what time it is much less the name of a street.

"Officer, I can explain," I began when the policewoman asked Greg for his license; she was wearing something not very subtle, a mixture of "White Shoulders" and leather. "I was just teaching my son how to drive; perhaps you ought to look at my license."

"Usually, most of the parental teaching around here is done in parking lots. And besides, your child does have to have a learners permit."

"I understand," I said to the officer and tried to look suitably contrite; she had one of those whiskey tenor voices I find so attractive in a woman plus a slight Irish lilt. "You see it's my weekend with my son—his mother and I divorced recently, and I was just trying to show him a good time. Perhaps, I ought to take over the driving?"

"Perhaps, you should. But first I'll have to see your license ... No, don't get out of the car." Apparently Greg, anxious to please, had begun to open his door. He shrank back in his seat, petrified, while I rolled down the window and prepared to hand the police officer my wallet.

"Would you take your license out of your wallet, Sir, and hand it to me?"

Oops. This was going to be a test. Where was my driver's license? End compartment. How to slip it out? Bottom? Side? Carefully, I slipped my fingers under the leather, light as a clumsy thief. Finally, I had it, not to panic. Gave the officer a bright smile as I handed it over.

"What's she doing?" Greg asked after we'd been left alone for several minutes.

"Probably running wants and warrants. Is she on the phone?"

"No." He moved about restlessly on the seat beside me searching for something to do with his now redundant arms and legs. My own distress was more internal, but just as real. What was she doing? Didn't they use radios any more? Had she already received some bad news?

Footsteps and the smell of "White Shoulders." "Thank you, Mr. Anders, I won't give you a ticket this time; I know how difficult divorce can be, but perhaps you ought to change drivers."

Quickly, I slipped out of the car and onto the pavement trying to look as brisk and business-like as I could. My fingertips reached out for the side panel to get my bearings.

"Your license, Sir. You'll want to put that back in your wallet."

Somewhere near me was an outstretched feminine hand with my license between its fingers. Where had the voice come from ... ah, a silhouette in the darkness. I reached out, felt the license in my palm, breathed, put the slim card back in my pocket. "Thank you officer."

Walk a few steps... where was the damn front of the car... turn; the front bumper hit my thigh; smile like Inspector Clouseau in the Pink Panther films. Carefully, around the front. Traffic streamed by in the adjacent lanes—asshole, you almost hit me—thankfully, it was late in the evening with few cars about. The traffic noises ceased, I stepped calmly around to the driver's side of the car and pulled open the door, fumbling only once for the handle. Greg pulled his own door open—had he been standing in the darkness by the curbside waiting to rescue me if I faltered—and when he sank back in the passenger seat, we both breathed a sigh of relief.

"White Shoulders" and leather again, leaning in the open driver's window. "You're blind aren't you?" I nodded my head. "Your ex-wife must be a real scum ball. Oops," she added as she realized my mythical ex-wife had to be Greg's mother. "Where do you live, Mr. Anders? Or may I call you Paul? I gather the address on your license is no longer correct."

"Avocado, just around the corner." At least, I hoped it was just around the corner. I'd been doing much too much hoping and sweating for the past half hour. "And please call me Paul."

"412," Greg added giving the Colombian's address, "It's an apartment."

"All right, son, what's your name?"

"Greg."

"All right Greg, I'm going to let you drive the car home. Only when you get there, no more driving, understood?"

Greg must have nodded his head, for she went on talking to him, "Now I want you to follow me. We'll be turning at the next corner and we may need to make quite a few turns. All right? Do you think you can do that?"

Greg and the policewoman apparently thought he could; I wasn't half so confident.

The officer came around one last time to my side of the car before we left. I rolled the window down and to my surprise she took my hand. "I'm Agnes Flattery, Paul. What apartment do you live in?"

"3C." I said, hoping this was not the Colombian's apartment.

"I may have to go on call before you actually get home," she said quietly, "Do you think the boy can do it?"

"Not a problem," I confided, lying.

"I may come back some evening to check on you, all right?" She pressed my fingers.

I stopped myself in the act of nodding obsequiously and gave her the killer smile instead. Only then did she release my hand. I like to think she was smiling back.

I felt like crying. I'd just given a potential bed companion a fake address.

Chapter 15

Agnes indeed was called away before we reached the apartment, so Greg informed me.

After a baffling series of turns—we apparently went in and out of some kind of expensive housing project (sure those two and three-story townhouses have 24-hour guard service and cost over a half mil each—still feels like a project to me)—we started down MacArthur back toward the ocean. Parking on Avocado proved next to impossible, at least near the bright lights that signaled the Colombian's ongoing party. I encouraged Greg to find a space where he could park at the rear of a line of cars—no way I'd be teaching parallel parking that night.

When we returned on foot to the Colombian's apartment, the street scene was much as it had been when we'd left an hour before. Girl was on the sidewalk with her erstwhile Colombian lover. Two pairs of feet wove an intricate duet on the pavement, but it was the Colombian alone who cooed to his desired mate in languid but impassioned Spanish. His words may well have been on the order of "Do not fly into the night my delicate pigeon, but stay here in the nest of my heart." I have no way of knowing; in contrast to a growing majority of Southern Californians, I don't speak or understand a syllable of the Hispanic language.

Girl introduced me to the Colombian as her "father," and Greg as her "younger brother." The Colombian, Armando was his name, assured me of his great respect for my daughter, though the activity of his hands once he discovered I was blind, Girl informed me, appeared to belie that.

Girl had a great deal to report, some of which actually had a bearing on our search. First, however, we had to listen to a dismal recital of Greg's and my own misdeeds, Greg having made some foolish remark early on about the difficulty of finding parking places in the area.

"You let him drive the car?" Girl repeated and then we had to go through our pathetic tale all over again. What had she thought we'd do when she left us alone that long? Call a taxi? (Why hadn't I thought of that before?)

Girl's own adventures had been a mixture of bravado, good fun, sexual gratification (limited, I gathered, to chaste kisses and the occasional Colombian trying to cop a feel), and intense fear.

"They beat up someone while I was there, just dragged him into a vacant bedroom and beat the hell out of him. Their apartment goes on and on. Could be four or even five of them living in the place with that many or more bedrooms. Expensive white leather furniture, glass tables, one table just for cutting lines of coke, a bar—'What did you have?' 'Rum and Coke.'—all sorts of languages, Spanish, English, German, Vietnamese. They mentioned the name of Greg's f-a-t-h-e-r."

"Greg's 13, he can spell," I reminded her.

"I know my father's a dope dealer." Greg said.

"But he's a dealer who doesn't deliver." Girl snickered. "Or rather, he doesn't pay for what he buys. Those guys were mad and scared, though they weren't talking about their fear in front of the other guests. I let Armando take me into a back bedroom, and we could hear what they were saying through the wall."

"You let him take you to a bedroom!"

"Don't shout boss. He said he wanted to show me some pre-Colombian statues."

"I'll bet. And what happened."

"Unless they get the money Greg's father owes them, they're in very big trouble with their own suppliers."

I slapped my fist on the dashboard interrupting her. "I meant what did you and Armando do in the back bedroom?"

"We kissed and Armando got to squeeze the merchandise, father."

"I'm not your father!" Was I shouting? Yes, I definitely was shouting.

"And just how old is Samantha?" Girl asked quietly, referring to my oldest daughter some eight years her senior.

We were silent for several moments; I could imagine Greg's head going back and forth between us like a spectator at a 19th century war wondering which of us would launch the next volley. The Volvo continued to roll smoothly over the pavement; no bumpty bump with Girl at the wheel. "Did you take Pacific Coast Highway?" I asked.

"Should I have?"

"Where are we now?"

"Almost at the 405. Pick a direction."

"Greg's father's place. Not where he lives, where he was hiding out. Rancho Santa Margarita."

"Shouldn't we take Greg home first?"

"Greg?" I said it quietly; gentle breathing from the back seat was the only reply.

"He must be sleeping."

"Wish I could." But I couldn't and didn't. I was caught up in life for a change, imagining my second meeting with Artie Clark. This time, I would get answers.

# Chapter 16

We didn't go to Artie's place. Cooler heads prevailed when we realized Greg would have to be in school the next morning. But Artie would be seeing us soon; he could count on it.

Going to my apartment meant having to pretend to be normal: clearing the couch so Greg could sleep on it, then waking him up again and having him take some sort of a shower.

"I take baths," he told me. Real men don't take baths. What did he want, some kind of rubber duck? Or maybe, he played with his GI Joe. Anyway, I didn't have a bathtub, just a shower equipped with all sorts of handles.

"You can sit on the floor by the drain," I told him. "Pretend it's a bath."

I made him use a washcloth and soap. At least, I draped the one over the shower stall and told him how to get the other out of its dispenser. Then I went and finished making up a bed on the couch. I didn't care if the sheets matched, though I knew Girl would be on my case in the morning.

"I like showers," he said, when he got out and was toweling himself dry. "I'm always going to take showers." A smart kid, one who just needed a father around to set a good example.

He was out like a light the minute he hit the sheets, his hair still wet. I threw a dry towel over it.

I wish I could have gone to sleep that easily. I tossed and turned worrying about the next morning; I worried about how we'd get Greg off to school; I worried about Donna. Artie, the little prick, had to know more than he'd been telling.

I though about what we'd done that day and about how Donna and I had met two evenings before: The dance at In Cahoots. The slow dance with Donna in my arms. Waking up,

Greg coming over on his bicycle. Where was the two-wheeler? I got up, found my thongs—I keep a half dozen pairs around so that a right and left will eventually turn up, and walked back out into the living room past the sleeping boy.

His bicycle was still out on the thin scrap of my lawn where he'd left it. I picked it up over a rose bush, scratching myself in the process, then rolled it over the doorstep into my living room. Back to bed, first toweling the dew off my feet.

Where was I? Greg coming over on his bicycle. We try to slip out of the apartments but Girl catches up with us. At his Dad's place we run into Lionel. Of all the people I'd met this one crowded day, Lionel had been the only one who was exactly what he seemed, and even he had tried to hold out on me. We'd met Artie, that sleezeball, and that nice couple he was staying with. Or could they really have been all that nice if they knew Artie? Probably a couple of dopers who didn't realize their friend was way beyond marijuana now and into the hard stuff. Their mother-in-law, no worse than my own, a combination of my mother for talk, my mother-in-law for sheer irritability. Miss you mom.

I had a cricket on my lawn just outside my window. Where had he come from? A faint scent of skunk drifted in on the breeze. Somewhere, some stupid cat was regretting having been so inquisitive.

Steady light breathing came from my front room, where a kid lay who trusted me to find his mom. I got up and did my breathing exercise. Calm your breathing, Sensei said, and you regain control.

What had I breathed that day? Roses, the light odor of Girl's sweat after her morning run, Donna, no that was the day before, gardenias in the church yard, gardenias again at the dance lesson, Brigitte's hand lotion, leather and "White Shoulders" and something indefinable in police officer Agnes's red hair—why had I given her a phony address? Then I, too, was sleeping.

I woke after the boy did. He'd already fixed himself a breakfast of toast and peanut butter, had found the milk and the pop-tarts, had even made a peanut butter sandwich for me. What he hadn't done was keep an eye on the clock or worry about turning in his homework. Fortunately, Girl woke in time to ask the sensible questions, and to drive us over to Greg's house, chasing after Greg who drove before us on his bicycle.

I wonder what the vaunted Mrs. Clara Hansen thought as she viewed this strange procession from her picture window.

Greg's homework was scattered here, there and everywhere. A better surrogate parent—Donna for sure had she been with us–would have made sure he organized it all the night before. As it was, we got him off to school, finally, after three false starts, including the need to package an apple and a Little Debbie Nutty Bar for his late morning snack.

"What next Paul?" Marci asked.

Next we searched the house, at least, Girl did while I followed her from room to room. Donna wore a padded bra and put potpourris wherever she could among her folded clothes. She did not have any narcotics hidden away in her closet; no room, anyway; it was packed end to end with blouses and pants on hangers. The only suspicious-looking box contained Christmas ornaments.

Greg kept a duplicate Frisbee in his room and an unending collection of Magic cards. At one time, he had really been interested in dinosaurs. Scale models filled his bureau top and one hung as a mobile from the ceiling. The only poster on his wall was that of Garth Brooks. What did we think we were looking for anyway?

Donna's little black book (it was actually beige) was in the kitchen in a drawer underneath the phone. I flipped through a couple of pages, then stuck it in my pocket for a later, more methodical perusal.

"What does Lionel want?" Marci asked stepping into the room.

"Lionel's got what he wants, that little sneak Artie."

"Then, why is he hanging around here?"

The best way to answer a question like that was to ask the man himself. I led Marci outside to where Lionel was sitting in his ancient Cadillac, engine running.

"Hi, Dr. Anders."

"Hi yourself. Why are you hanging around Donna's place?"

"'Cause I think this is where he hid the dope or the money or both."

I didn't have to ask who "he" was. "Artie doesn't live here."

Marci was more helpful. "We just searched the house and didn't find anything. But you're welcome to look."

"We can't let him inside. Donna wouldn't like that."

"Paul, you're acting like a jealous fool. You're not her husband. You're not even her boyfriend, really. If Lionel wants to look, let him look."

"Who's the boss here," I began, though the answer to that question was already obvious.

Back in together we trooped, though Marci said she had a class to go to. I wasn't going to leave Lionel inside alone and I sure wasn't going to let him scatter stuff all over. He did help though, looking in places that neither Marci nor I would have thought of looking. Still, he didn't come up with anything Marci and I hadn't already found, unless you count a magazine with pictures of nude women that Lionel found at the back of Greg's closet. It belonged to Artie, probably. He seemed the type that would share something like that with his son.

"Paul, I've got to go to class."

So that's how I ended up driving back with Lionel and going out with him for a burger later, forgetting all about that phone book of Donna's that I was carrying around in my back pocket.

## Chapter 17

Don't ever attack a blind man, not if you think he might know how to fight.

Run him down with a car, maybe; honk the horn at the last moment and he might just jump in the wrong direction. But don't try to tackle him head on. Once you move in close enough, you stand as good a chance of being nailed by him as he does of being creamed by you.

Nobody had clued Frank in on this. Also, no one had told him not to wear shaving lotion if you're going to hide in the bushes or at least not to wear the same shaving lotion that you wear everyday.

None of the preceding should suggest that our struggle that evening was one sided or that if I had my druthers Frank would have stayed home and watched Seinfeld reruns. We traded blow for blow and in the end I had enough bruises to make the rest of the evening extremely uncomfortable.

After dinner, I like to take a brief walk around the neighborhood, my block of it anyway, and see how the neighbor's gardens are doing. I can imagine a day when Donna might take that walk with me. The Williams have roses and have recently planted a few other scented varieties specifically for me.

Frank was waiting at the end of my walkway, revenge in mind, and as I approached stepped out directly in my path. He would have been just a huge gray blob between me and the lamppost if it hadn't been for the shaving lotion and the fist that came whizzing out to greet me. I stepped in toward him and slightly to the side. "Stoime," the technique is called and is supposed to be effective even with sword strokes. I could only wish the walkway provided just a little more room for lateral movements and the downward pivot that is characteristic of Aikido. It doesn't, so I kicked out at about knee height, caught his leg and scraped my shoe down along it till I crushed his instep. He grabbed me around the rib cage and squeezed; I stuck my fingers in his eyes. He threw punches, and I threw punches. We were pretty much even up, except I had the longer reach.

He rushed in and got kicked where it hurts. My next few punches hit his face and upper body, but I couldn't count on too many repetitions. A right hook of mine contacted thin air because he'd stepped back.

The narrow walkway was a problem for both of us. No dodging to the side unless one wanted to absorb a thorn in his cheek. A final kick on my part caught him in the backside so I guess he'd given up and was running away.

A woman cried out, "Hey you, stupid." Then Frank was gone and the woman stood next to me saying, "Crazy person ran away." Miss Wu had come to visit.

# Chapter 18

My immediate reaction to Miss Woo's suggestion that I go with her to a concert was to provide a firm and irrevocable, "no." Had this invitation been delivered over the telephone, this is exactly what I would have said. But not only did Woo make her invitation in person, she did it with Marci looking on; that took guts. I can remember those moments of stark terror when I began to ask girls out on dates. Moments not that distant come to think of it.

I should say that by the time the invitation was given, we'd all gone back inside my apartment. The onlookers, mainly tenants from my building along with Marci and Greg had dispersed. I'd been checked for injuries, a minor cut on my arm bandaged (the rose bushes got me) and I'd taken a couple of aspirin as a precautionary measure.

With a glass of water and just a drop or two of brownish liquid inside me, I was ready to answer questions and respond to invitations.

So I delayed the "no" for a moment or two and asked Woo, "What kind of concert?" I'd a number of stock answers ready to give her in reply: "Country music? Okay to dance to, but I can't stand to listen to it." "Rock? Yeah, maybe if I didn't have to sit in a seat; in my day, we could get up and walk around. But what Miss W. said was, "It's a symphony my friend Chen Yi composed." A western-style symphony written by a Chinese woman sounded just crazy enough to be interesting.

After ensuring that Greg had done his homework—no, he wouldn't mind being left alone, he and Marci would make out okay, and that Marci would look in on him—"He's fourteen boss, not eight," I allowed myself to be led up the steps from my apartment and down the walk to Miss Woo's Audi.

Miss Woo seemed determined I would put on my seat belt before she would start the car. Though I had almost figured out how the straps worked, she reached across and adjusted them for me.

"I'm never going to learn if you help me."

"I can touch you this way," she whispered.

Great; simply great.

Someone tapped on the passenger-side window. I was fumbling for the handle so I could talk with them, when Miss Woo rolled down the window for me.

Marci leaned in and we banged heads. "Boss, I've something I need to tell you. I couldn't at dinnertime, not with Greg present. That woman—the one you met at the church, she was outside Greg's home this morning.

"Why didn't you say something?"

"I didn't recognize her at first. She had a small child with her and was pushing a baby carriage."

"She probably lives in the neighborhood. She and Donna go to the same church." I was conscious of the pair of ears in the driver's seat next to me; small and dainty to be sure, still they had to be listening to every word Marci and I said.

"When I drove around the comer, she was loading the carriage into the back of a mini-van. Boss, she did not have a baby in the back of that carriage, just a doll. I know because she handed it to her little girl."

"She must be detective." Miss Woo, never the shy one, had decided to get involved. I decided to leave and fumbled for the door handle.

"Boss. Stay. Enjoy yourself."

"We need to talk to that woman."

"I can do it. Ill track her down, find out where she lives."

"You're supposed to be watching Greg."

"First thing in the morning."

74

"Please." But we'd only just pulled away from the curb when I began having second thoughts. Had we done all we could to find Donna that day? Looked everywhere we should look?

Miss Woo's good spirits weren't at all daunted by my silence, not with a subject or three she felt compelled to chatter on about—classical music, careers for the blind and the sighted, importance of family, her childhood in Taiwan. And where had I been raised? A long time ago in quite a different place. And where had I been since? Here and there, a summer in Chicago, a year at Fort Ord (I taught at the Officer's College, I wasn't in the service), two years in New Orleans, six in the Bay area. But her question was just an excuse for her to say in turn, "I was educated in Kansas," say it with pride as if I didn't know from the film that Kansas was in black and white.

I tuned out her prattle, but I couldn't tune out thoughts of Miss Woo completely. What had I been told? A pretty face by western standards, not much in the way of a bust, but significant headlights. The last time she called on me, she'd worn a soft bra and a transparent white blouse. Could meaning be read into that? What if Marci hadn't been with me? What if Miss Woo hadn't worn any clothes at all? I held the thought, even though I knew by now that having descended from the freeway we were traversing the war zone that led into downtown LA. Metal shutters walled off the shops, closed for the night. The homeless had dragged out their cardboard boxes, half to be used for shelter and half for fuel.

And still, when a sensible person would have been thought only about locking car doors and responding to armed intruders, I continued to think of Donna and Miss Woo in the nude.

My brain wasn't the only body part involved in the process. Always one to speak her mind, Woo said as we pulled into our parking slot, "Goodness, look how you sticking up through your pants. We can't have that."

We can't? Are erections strictly forbidden at classical music concerts? Or was she thinking of the earlier moments when we would cross the street, ascend the stairs to the concert hall, and line up in front of the ticket booth? Would she be embarrassed giving a quarter to a homeless man, when her escort had an erection? Not to worry Woo; by the time I am introduced to your friend Chen Yi, all will be at peace again.

But the ultra-thorough, ultra-crazed Miss W was taking no chances. With the same ease with which she had earlier tied my safety belt, she reached down and grabbed my belt with one hand and unzipped me with the other. Were my innermost parts not to be kept secret from paid agents of the State of California? Of course, in bending down and applying her mouth to my swollen member, Miss Woo may well have been acting on her own volition.

The process, alas, was over much too soon, a product of my own recent abstinence and Miss Woo's relentless efficiency. The first would no doubt be tempered by repetition. What, if anything, might be done about the latter, ought be considered at a later time.

We made our way through the crowd of panhandlers that surrounded the hall without incident and picked up our tickets at the box office. Miss Woo did know someone as our tickets were already paid for.

I would like to be able to tell you that the subsequent concert represented a successful merger of East and West (or at least as successful as the encounter in the car beforehand), but I found Chen Yi's music terribly strange, at least at first hearing.

Traditional western instruments played not altogether familiar scales. From time to time in among the flutes and violins came the strange sounds of instruments that I, at least, had never heard before. Dying whales rose among the bassoons and oddly tuned drums sounded in among the more familiar timpani and chimes.

Afterward, we did meet with Chen Yi and I lied gracefully concerning my appreciation of her music. "She is so fat," Miss Woo whispered in my ear, which I suppose meant Chen Yi was at best pleasingly plump, Miss Woo's standards of shape and size being based on her own somewhat spare body.

Back in the parking lot, she failed to start the car. "Too much traffic," she said and put her hand in exploratory fashion on my thigh. The results must have been adequate for she soon had me unzipped a second time. "The traffic," I cautioned but to no avail. Shifting headlights flickered this way and that through our windows, unnerving me enough that Miss Woo was able to work her will for some time without visible results.

"Now, you must please me," she said and grabbing my hand, inserted it proudly between her legs. She continued to provide voluminous instructions concerning my subsequent actions, even locking my wrist in place with her hand to make sure that timbre and tempo remained on beat. When she was finally and fully satisfied, the pungent odor of litchi having overtaken that of apple blossom, my hand and arm were both wet—I'd come myself during the process to add to her substantial contribution. Not only was the last of the flickering headlights well on its way clear of the downtown area but even the lights in the parking lot had been turned off. For whatever reason, the crazed junkies that inhabit the night had chosen to let us alone.

"You are a very good love," she said.

I remained silent on the trip home, thinking and not thinking, though perhaps I ought to have said "thank you" to the lady. By contrast, Miss Woo was every bit as voluble as she'd been on the trip into town. High school, florist, partner, family, children were the words she chose to reorganize my life.

My thoughts, scattered and intermittent, were of Donna. Was she okay? What could we do that we hadn't done so far? Where could we look? In the morning, I would find her. I had to.

# Chapter 19

In the morning, once I'd got Greg off to school, my only thoughts were of myself. You'd think a man who'd gotten his cock blown, not once but twice, by a passably decent woman (an amateur anyway) would have thoughts that were upbeat and positive. My thinking processes went just the other way.

I just didn't seem to have many choices any more. My realization of this brought me down, way down.

Miss Woo was certainly not a woman I'd have chosen as a sex partner, not even for a quick bit on the side. Her personality ruled against it. But when you're blind, you have to go with the flow. You can't count on people or doorways being available when you want them. People don't treat you just like the next guy, because you're not like the next guy, anymore.

I wear dark glasses, sometimes, even though I have partial sight, simply to cover up the scar tissue around my eyes. I've a funny scar across my forehead, also; it feels and probably looks more like plastic than like skin. The surgeons inserted a hair plug just above the scar. It hasn't fallen out but the surrounding hair has never grown long enough to cover the gash.

I live with what I have, but I'm not completely happy, yet.

I once had a wife and three children. Two of the children wouldn't speak to me after the divorce. Never mind that I was in Atlanta when the bomb exploded because I'd gone to see one of them compete in the Olympics. Sure, they spoke to me afterward, but we had nothing to say.

My third and youngest child was there for me every moment, spending far too much time at the hospital and later during my not-yet-complete therapy. Then one day, me under the covers, she at bedside sitting upright in her usual straight chair, I told her to get a life, get back to her own career, find a man, settle down. She told me she had a fiancé, she'd had one for some time, they'd just been waiting for me to recover to get married.

They got married—I gave the bride away; he took her to live with him on the other side of the country, almost as far away as you could go. So, now I was like a salmon that had spawned. What purpose did I have? No goals, no further falls to jump, I could just live off my fat, until the shriveled, uncaring remnant of my former self faded away.

I'd seen my grandfather do that. One day, big and healthy, the next, having fallen from a tractor, old and sick, until finally he caught pneumonia and died. Grandmother played bridge with her friends every weekday until she was ninety-two. She fractured her hip—"I was just reaching for a glass on the sink."—went to the hospital, went from a semi-private room to a convalescent home, and then she, too, was gone.

"You're not ninety-two, Dad," my daughter said on the telephone. "You're barely midway through your fifties."

"My father, your grandfather, died from a stroke when he was sixty-five."

"And you've got medicines and well-trained doctors, he never dreamed of. You don't eat meat, not often; you've lain off the twinkles and the fatty foods. Give yourself forty more years, maybe forty-five if you stay on the diet Carlis gave you."

Doing what for forty years, I asked myself. What does an aging salmon do? Who does he do it with?

I had an offer in my lap, of course, Miss Woo. But I also had a dream, a warm loving woman with a teen-age son. The woman was missing. I would find her. I would live my dream.

# Chapter 20

Shouldn't Greg be home?

What gets us through many of the low spots in our life—for all of us suffer from depression from time to time–is the realization that we have too many responsibilities to stay down for long.

Kids, a dog, even a goldfish keep us alive, keep us from putting a razor to our wrists, a quick bullet through the head. When we've someone who depends on us, we forget how depressed we are, we do what must be done.

The chiming clock above the piano told me that school was out, that Greg should be back at my apartment. They, the Colombians or someone else, had kidnapped Donna to put pressure on Artie, why not Greg as well? I telephoned Donna's house, it was Greg's real home after all. No one answered. I telephoned his school; a boy's soccer game was being played that day. Did Greg play soccer? Maybe. Where was the field? More important, how would I get there?

Marci wasn't home. Her classes wouldn't be out for several hours yet. Should I ask a neighbor for a lift? Call a cab? The county provides free transport for the blind, but only if you phone 24 hours in advance.

On the sidewalk outside my apartment—I would walk, if Greg could bike over, it couldn't be all that far—I ran into Miss Woo. "Your pants don't match," she said. I explained I had no time to change; as usual, she was not to be reasoned with.

Inside the apartment, she tried to take advantage of my brief pantless state. This time, I was not to be reasoned with. "You no want me to touch?" I had to find Greg.

Miss Woo gave me a lift in her immaculate Audi. At first, I thought her helping me was because she reasoned once the crisis was over I would be more amenable to her overtures. But, of course, she too needed a purpose, needed to feel fulfilled.

We reached the soccer fields and made our way slowly from junior varsity to varsity and back to frosh-soph. Each time I would ask the coach, once we'd located him and got his attention, whether Greg was at the practice. Greg plays basketball we learned from one of the players at the frosh-soph field. The score was 1–1 as the teams broke for the half, both sides excited, convinced they might still win.

Back to the school gym we went in lockstep. I was grateful now that Miss Woo was there, that I had someone to guide me, to locate and ask questions of strangers. But the gym was closed. A young Asian boy asked if we'd tried the park.

"Let's go to his house, first," I said. Perhaps Greg was at his home now, had found the note I'd left on his door and gone inside to wait as instructed. Or perhaps…?

"He lives with your wife?" Miss Woo questioned. I explained I wasn't married, that Greg wasn't really my boy. "Then how come he stay with you?"

This seemed too complicated to explain or, maybe, by now frightened of all the possibilities, I wanted to keep Miss Woo in reserve, someone to fall back on if I never saw Donna again.

The door to Greg's home was locked and no one answered our knock. "Ask neighbor." Woo walked next door to where the elderly couple lived. Greg had been home; perhaps he was at the park. And a woman from Donna's church had come by, looking for her.

"Probably Diane," Woo said.

How on earth could Miss Woo possibly know the name of someone who knew Donna? "You know her. We went dancing. We have long talk afterward.

"You and Marci speak about her last night."

Something clicked then and I put the name and image together. Diane was my sanctimonious Christian friend, the one who been accompanying the Reverend on his visits to Donna, the one who had gone spying the previous morning on her own. "Why didn't you tell us about this last night, Woo?"

Any reply remained unvoiced.

Fortunately, wee met Greg halfway to the park, riding on his bicycle with Girl, tall on her mountain bike, riding beside him.

He'd been to my home, been back and forth to his, met Girl at my place, now here they were. I pulled him against my shoulder, rubbed his head, almost kissed him. I loved this kid. Or perhaps I missed that time when I had my own children, just Greg's size, needing me as much as he needed me now.

# Chapter 21

Girl said, "I've something to tell you."

"I'll bet you have. Why didn't you follow up on that woman with the baby carriage the way you promised?" Never mind that I hadn't followed up either, had lain in bed half the day feeling sorry for myself.

"But I did. I found out what she's up to or what she thinks she's up to." Girl paused as if expecting me to interrupt once again. Sensibly, I said nothing. "It took a lot less time to track her down than I thought it would. Of course, I could have used the time studying.

"I went to the church. It was closed, but a group of older ladies were sunning themselves on the front porch. One reminded me of my grandmother. They told me that during the week, the church is a senior citizen's center. Or, maybe it's the other way around; the center rents out its rooms on the weekend for use as a church.

"'Could they help me find the New Christians?' They didn't know but I could ask Teacher.

"Teacher was a ditz; she was less organized than you are, Boss, and she wasn't much younger than the senior citizens on the porch. It took almost ten minutes for her to tell me the New Christians only used the building on Sundays, and she wasn't sure, but she thought the lady in the blue and gray house next door might have a key.

"The house next door had yellow paint; fortunately, one of the gray-haired ladies was able to point me in the right direction. The woman I was looking for lived three doors down in a pale green house with a border of lantanas, and had the most darling children ages five, seven, and eight."

Get to the point, I thought, but again said nothing. I suppose Marci wanted me to appreciate how much work she'd done on my behalf. I'd appreciate it only if it helped me find Donna.

"I walked over and knocked on the pale green door of the pale green house. It was your friend from the church all right. Dolled up in a sleeveless white dress. The dress may have been intended to show off her tan, but weighing what she does, all I could think was put it back in the can, sister."

"Fat." Miss Woo interjected.

"Hefty, maybe, or plump. More on top than on the bottom. Boss likes that. One thing I don't understand. She's got a scarf wrapped around her head to keep the dust out of her hair while she cleans, but she's wearing a white sleeveless dress. White's a magnet for dirt.

"Great eyes, green irises like a cat, and lips–I wish I had lips that good, but no make up. A little make-up wouldn't hurt to set her features off.

"We stare at each other for a full half minute before she whips off the headscarf.

"I tell her my name, but she doesn't tell me what her name is. I tell her I have a few things I need to discuss with her. She says she isn't sure she has time to talk. A little dark-haired girl pokes her head out of a doorway about halfway down the hall. She's the same little girl I saw outside Greg's home yesterday, the one with the doll. I wink and the head disappears. 'Are you married?' I ask the woman. Don't ask what made me think of the question.

"'Of course.' She flashes her ring, but it only makes me more suspicious.

"Then where's your husband?'

"'He's not here.' Her voice isn't defensive, but the way she crosses her arms across her chest is. The little girl pokes her head out the doorway again, and I make it a point not to look at her. When she sees me not looking as hard as I can, she giggles.

"Is he at work?' I venture.

"The woman nods; I can tell she's holding her breath.

"What does he do?'

"'He's a carpenter.'

"'He's not in town?'

"'No.' She blushes and looks away. Guilty: in her own mind, at least. The little girl had come out to be with her mother and she puts an arm around her in kind of a hug without looking down.

"'How long has he been out of town?' I ask.

"'Five years.'"

"'Not much of a marriage.'

"The Reverend says,' she begins, then makes a funny little movement with her mouth, not finishing the sentence. I guess she knows how little I care for the Reverend's opinion. 'I'm married,' she repeats. Obviously, she's trying to convince herself more than me.

"'And just why did you visit Donna yesterday?'

"'Why to talk with her. Just to talk.'

"'About?'

"'About her marriage.'

'I make a motion with my hand for the woman to keep talking. She blushes and looks guilty again. I wonder if she knows she's squeezing her child's hand. 'That was all,' she persists.

"Liar, liar, pants on fire. 'No, it wasn't.'

"'You're not even a member of our church.'

"I could see myself trying to explain that to you, Boss. 'What was the real reason you went to see Donna?'

"'She has something she was keeping for the Reverend. An address book; she has the addresses of all the members of our congregation.'

86

"'Have you slept with him?' I ask.

"'Who?' she replies. The blush takes its time spreading across the acre of exposed skin. She answers, 'Who?' not 'no,' Boss. Definitely not the response I'd expect from someone as married as she claims to be.

"'May I come in?' I ask.

"You may not.'

"'Will you come out? I'd like you to take me to this Reverend.' Actually, I'd rather kiss a pig. The things I do for you, Boss.

"She blushes again. 'He's not home.'

"'He has a home of his own then, does he?'

"''Yes, he has a home.'

"She's got her child in front of her now as a barrier and her arms crossed in front of the child. Time to go. I've learned something, I think. Even if I'm still not sure what. It wasn't all time wasted.

"Thank you Miss, uh, Miss...' I pause so the woman can fill in her name.

"'Mrs.' And she closes the door without saying anything more.

"So what do you want to do now, Boss? Take Greg home? Visit her again? Track down the Reverend?"

"I want to come," Greg said.

I ignored him. I also ignored Miss Woo, who had linked her arm in mine sometime earlier and kept pressing against my side.

"Maybe it's time I looked in Donna's address book."

Chapter 22

Donna's little black book had been pieced together over many years and may even have dated to before her marriage. Marci flipped through its pages quickly, before launching a second more methodical inspection. Arizona phone numbers predominated as well as a few from California. I would guess Donna's maiden name had been Tewksbury.

Artie Clark's number had been crossed out and replaced again and again. Two of his numbers remained untouched. One in ballpoint was a local exchange, probably the unpainted house in Westminster we'd visited yesterday. The second, more recent addition was in pencil. Girl dialed the number then turned the phone over to me.

"Hello?" A young woman's voice, shaky, hadn't had her morning fix.

"I'm calling about the curtains." It was the first thing that came into my mind.

"The curtains?"

"Who are you talking to? Who's on the phone?" an officious older woman's voice demanded to know in the background. I recognized this voice, both voices now that I thought about it: The couple Artie was staying with, the wife and the mother-in-law.

"Artie?" I said after I hung up the phone, and then, translating my thoughts into a more tangible whole for Girl's benefit, "Donna's got the phone number where Artie's been staying the last couple of days; she's had it all along."

Chapter 23

The homeowners of the Rancho Santa Margarita hillside
community were all tucked away for the night, garage doors
down, sprinklers silenced; the blue glow filtering through the
curtains from their televisions were the only signs of life
within.

The T.V. screen shone in Artie's friends' living room also,
but somehow, I didn't think the friends were home. Artie was;
we'd found his car parked up on the hilltop where Artie had
been hiding in it the day before.

"How will we get in?" Girl wanted to know.

"Bimbo in distress, the usual." I replied.

"He's seen me before."

I threw my hands in the air. "You've changed outfits.
Besides, he was focussed on Lionel when we were here last.
Just try not to show him your face. Oh, and take off your bra."

"Boss!" But she slipped off her brassiere as ordered,
fumbling beneath her dress. I just hoped Greg found the
change instructive.

I had directions for him, too. "Greg, I want you to stand
down the street at the end of the block where you'll be barely
visible under the last street light. Your Dad will be able to see
you, but won't be able to tell who you are." (And you'll be well
out of the line of fire. I thought but did not say.)

Girl jogged in place, both to get herself psyched up and to
make her breathing sound as if she'd had to run the last few
blocks. She finished the job by running up the path to the
house and pounding on the door.

"Help me please!" she called and when no answer came
from inside, she shouted again. Artie came to the front door,
opened it but did not remove the chain. What value this thin

metal barrier would have against hard cases like the Colombians was uncertain, but nobody so far had accused Artie Clark of an excess of smarts.

"A man's chasing me," Girl puffed.

"Where?" Artie asked suspiciously

Girl pointed off down the street to where Greg was standing.

"Why he's smaller than you are," Artie said, "big girl like you ought to be able to take care of yourself. Good looking, too. Well, c'mon in and I'll take care of you."

"Creep, I'd rather take my chances with him," Girl howled and started back up the path. Artie slipped the chain and followed quickly after. I grabbed him just as he reached the corner of the house.

"Inside."

"Hey." He complained continuously, but was no match for the two of us.

"Kitchen," I said to Girl and in a moment we were in the elaborate kitchen. "Sit," I said, and then to Girl, "Looks like a nice place."

"All electric," she said. "Big chopping block, pots and pans on the walls."

"I'll need a knife," I said, "a simple pairing knife will do, but it has to be sharp."

"Hey, what do you guys want with me? I know you, you're the blind guy from yesterday morning."

"Pin his arm," I said to Girl, studiously ignoring his comment.

"We want to know where Donna is."

"I told you yesterday, I don't know."

"Ah, but that was yesterday. Pin his arm." Sensing that Greg had entered the room and was standing behind me in the doorway, I turned and told him to go back to the car.

"Greg, don't let them hurt me."

"Tell them where Mom is, Dad."

"Amazingly enough," I said, ignoring Artie's protests, and lecturing just as if I were back in my familiar anatomy laboratory, "removing the skin from a primate is not much different than peeling a stalk of celery. You need a sharp knife—this knife is sharp isn't it, and then you just run it along the limb with a swift cut angled close to the skin."

Artie fainted and Greg gave a low moan. "Greg, wait outside. Girl, get me a glass of water." But she'd anticipated me and was already pouring the water over Artie's head.

"Ouch," Artie said sitting up and almost fainting a second time when he saw the raw meat of his arm, the long sliver of skin still adhering to it at the end of the cut. "How are you going to put that back?"

"I wasn't planning to reassemble you Artie. I'm an anatomy professor, not a surgeon. We usually operate on corpses."

"She's down in the canyon," Artie said, "Greg's mom. I've got a cabin down on the canyon floor. I tied her up. But I was just doing it to protect her."

Our faces revealed our disbelief.

"Honestly."

I picked up the knife a second time. "Tell us how to get there." Artie did. Just in case he might be lying, we left him tied securely on his back in a rear bedroom, then trooped outside to join Greg on the pavement.

Following the Thomas Guide to the very edge of Santa Margarita, which proved to be only several blocks away, we looked down on a jeep trail that led to the bottom of a canyon. "I'm not taking the Volvo down that," Girl said.

"We'll walk then."

"No lights," Greg complained.

"Follow me. Pretend you're part of a Brueghel painting."

"One moment," Girl said, and we could hear her thrashing about in the underbrush. When she returned she thrust some kind of cane into my hands.

"What is this?" I marveled. Firm, strong, lightweight; she'd broken off the central stalk of a Yucca plant for use as a guide in the darkness.

"You and Greg could use canes, too," I suggested, "help you to stay on the path, keep you from walking into things."

"We'll just follow you," she said, "The way we've been doing."

"Do you always need the last word?"

Now, she was silent.

Vegetation overhung the sides of the trail, with tufts of grass and small stones everywhere underfoot. The air smelled of fresh earth, nightcrawlers, the moistness of frogs and insect-eating plants. The cracked pavement was good for the first fifteen yards before giving way to dirt. "Lucky it hasn't rained, we'd be getting our feet caught in the ruts."

"Slow down," Girl said, which I thought was interesting coming from her. A couple of times, I led my group into the underbrush amid the manzanita and mesquite when the trail turned faster than I did, but on the whole, it was a safe, if not a quick, trip down.

What we needed now was luck. The trails on the bottom seemed to lead everywhere among the willows and acacia. The waning moon, low on the horizon, had already abandoned the canyon. Girl and Greg wouldn't be much help to me.

I'd forgotten the nightlights of the city. "That way," Girl said, gripping my arm. "I see something shiny to your left near the ground. Could be a propane tank. And you can see the outline of a cabin."

"I'll let you go in first then."

"No thanks, but I'll be right behind you."

An owl screamed in the distance and a wood rat ran through the underbrush just off to our right. We could hear the faint creek of branches shifting in the wind, and the soft chirrup of some happy tree frogs.

"Spiders!" Cobwebs entangled in my fingers as I groped about me with my yucca stem. I'd found the side window of the cabin, apparently. The front door was an easy find, too, though I had to break a pane to get at the locked handle from inside. "I think someone is in there. What can you see through the window?"

"Too dark to tell," Girl whispered.

"I'll go in," Greg said. Maybe he was being especially brave; maybe he just didn't want to stand around in the darkness with the spiders.

"I'll go," I said and opened the door.

I'd lived in the country once up in back of Pasadena in a canyon much like this one, more civilized even. One evening, I'd stepped out my side door wearing only a pair of rubber sandals, stepped on a rattle snake and in an instant demonstrated that those animated cartoons in which the character runs along madly several feet above the ground are entirely consistent with known physical laws.

I also beat the hell out of that rattlesnake with a spade once I hit the ground.

Snakes might not be scattered over the floor of this cabin, but I walked slowly and carefully as if there were, my made-to-order cane tapping its way before me. When I found the opening to the kitchen, I sensed rather than heard the sound of someone in the far corner trying to stifle his or her breathing.

Donna," I ventured and received a joyous if inarticulate, "Phiff" in reply. To hell with the rattlesnakes! I crossed the kitchen in three quick strides, tripped over something on the floor, spilling it—the bowl for the cat, I learned later, and almost knocked Donna over.

She was tied to a chair, her wrists bound behind her, a cloth gag covering her mouth. I untied the gag first, my hands gentle on her hair, and then set to work on the knots on her wrists even as she was saying, "Oh God, you're my hero, thank you, thank you," and crying.

When the lights came on—I'd not even thought about looking for a switch, that's the way Marci and Greg found us, Donna in my arms, me learning that when the breath smells like ripe peaches, that's exactly the way the mouth tastes.

# Chapter 24

Outside the cabin, Greg and his mom had a long hugging session with Greg seeming to gain years and inches with each hug. Donna only said, "that Asshole," when she learned Artie had not told Greg where she was.

Artie had called her the night before saying he was in trouble and then, when she'd come to his aid—"Never, never again"—he'd tied her up in the cabin telling her guys were out looking for him and he didn't want them to hurt her by mistake. I didn't try to disabuse her, not with Greg listening to every word.

We made it back though the woods okay, Donna wondering how we could have come that far without a flashlight. "We've got one in the kitchen."

Before the others could turn back, Greg cried out, "I see lights!"

"Where?" his mother asked; she gripped my hand tightly.

"At the top of the trail." Girl answered for him, "Could be as many as half a dozen people, Boss." But I could already hear the voices echoing in the silence and see the flickers of light at the edges of my vision.

I yawned; not out of boredom, not when God knows what was heading down the canyon toward us, but from exhaustion. Since the explosion, I'd sort of got used to the sedentary life—staying in bed in the morning because I had no real reason for rising, then going to bed earlier than I needed to because I had no real reason for staying up. This day just didn't seem to have an end. I yawned again.

Wake up self. Wake up everybody.

"We'll go up the trail as far as we can," I said, "until just before they can see us, and then we'll head out to the side of the path into the underbrush."

"How do we know when 'it's just before they can see us?'"

"You decide," I replied, trusting Girl with my life and the lives of my new family once again.

We were tucked safely behind a rock on the hillside when the procession reached us. We'd had only one bad moment searching for a hiding place, when Donna stepped on a fallen branch and thought it was a snake. "I see Armando," Marci said.

The sad-looking scarecrow the Colombians dragged behind them along the path was Greg's father. Greg made a move to rise, but I restrained him, holding him closely until the procession had passed.

"He's really not a bad guy," Donna began once they were out of earshot, and then stopped abruptly, not being sure herself, I suppose, what Artie's good points were.

I could hear Girl snort in the background. "He locked you up in that cabin, tied you to a chair."

"He only did that so they wouldn't be suspicious, really. He came down as often as he could and then he'd bring me food or sit and talk with me."

"And Greg," Girl said. "Your boy was worried sick."

"I don't understand about that part. Artie said he would telephone Greg."

"Well he didn't." Girl and I said together.

"He didn't, mama," Greg chimed in. I noticed again that the poise and polish that had characterized him the day we met still came and went in flashes. Once again, he was a frightened little boy in desperate need of his parent. Thankfully, he now had her.

"Twice when we confronted Artie, he denied knowing anything at all about your whereabouts."

"He was just trying to protect me."

"He's the guy who led them to you in the first place."

Girl snorted a second time. I was too disgusted and tired to care one way or the other. Greg just kicked at the ground.

"Do you love him?" Girl asked Donna.

"He is the father of my child."

"Do you love him?"

"No."

"Then let's get out of here. Soon as they figure out no one is in the cabin, they'll kill him and be back lickety split up the path."

At last, an idea I thought we could all agree on.

"He's my husband," Donna said, stubbornly. "I mean he was. I'd like to know what's going on down there."

Girl's mouth opened but emitted only a gulp; she kicked at the ground angrily, raising a spray of pebbles; I could hear them tumbling down the hillside.

"Mama, we've got to save him."

Another country heard from.

"Not you Greg. I can't let you go. I can't lose you honeybunch."

So who was supposed to go? Girl and I?

"This is dumb," Girl said five minutes later as we stumbled down the path.

"I promised Donna."

"You promised her what? That we'd rescue her scumbag ex, kill six or eight Colombians with our bare hands, and somehow whisk Artie to safety?"

"He's Greg's father." I persisted stubbornly.

Girl took me by the shoulders and put her face only a few inches from mine. "What are we supposed to do?"

"Watch."

"And you're blind!" When she spoke again a moment later, her voice was subdued, tired. We were both so tired. "I'm sorry Boss."

She hugged me. I hugged her back. We took two more stumbling steps downward.

Chapter 25

The Colombians weren't expecting visitors. They made no secret of their presence, barking out curses in rapid Spanish as they ripped up Artie's cabin looking for the cocaine. Flashlight beams were shooting every which way, so we had to crawl most of the last hundred yards.

When we were almost at the cabin, Girl pulled on my pant leg. I lay still, awaiting her directions, wondering why she'd had to stop just where a large rock would be pressing in my side. "Gumpf," she whispered; then, realizing she was talking to the wrong end of my body, she moved headward and repeated, "They've started a fire."

I tilted my head at an awkward angle and looked back at the cabin. Not my imagination then—those flickers of light were flames. Fools. This was Southern California in the dry season. It would take only minutes for the fire to spread throughout the canyon. To hell with concealment, to hell with finding Artie, we had to get away.

"Wait!" Marci called. The noise from behind us grew louder. "Now, they're trying to put it out."

"I wish them luck," I whispered, "let's get out of here."

But we were too late: the fire had spread to the bushes. Only the lack of wind kept it from climbing immediately up the sides of the canyon. It would create its own wind soon, a product of the fire's heat, would spread and consume everything in its path.

The Colombians had stopped shouting, were staring in awe at the flames. I pulled on Girl's leg. "Let's get the hell out of here."

"I've got to help them put it out."

"We have got to call the fire department."

Girl stood up, but not to come with me. I could here her tearing a dead branch from a nearby tree. What was she going to do, use it as a shovel?

I sensed the presence of others on the canyon floor, heard Armando trying to explain something in his halting English to a newcomer, heard a portable generator start up, and the sound of water spraying from a hose. How much good would a single hose do?

At the same time as the fires around the cabin were finally quenched, a tall willow to the left suddenly burst into flame. Its light, incredibly bright, would have seared the retinas of those nearby.

For an instant, I thought selfishly: they'll see me sitting here, they'll come and hurt me. Someone, probably one of the neighbors from the canyon called, "Don't give up," and again I heard the sound of shovels and people running about on the canyon floor.

Sparks leapt about us and one could smell the green wood burning. I started up the hillside.

"Did you see Artie?" Donna asked the minute I returned.

"I tried to help." Greg said, "She wouldn't let me."

"I wouldn't let you, sweetheart. Mama doesn't want you to get hurt.

"Where's your friend?" Donna asked abruptly.

I had no idea where Girl was, somewhere below us still digging at the ground with her damned stick. Was I crying?

Donna touched my arm. "It'll be okay," she said. "I think they've put out the fire. Marci will be back soon."

Footsteps could be heard running up the nearby trail passing the point where we were hiding. "Here," I called, indifferent to whether I'd be heard by the Colombians. If it were Marci, I wanted to see her now.

It was Marci, first the voice, then the smell, mostly of wood smoke, then a hand, an arm, all of her in my arms. "You, okay, Paul?" she said with the breath I hadn't squeezed from her.

"Am I okay? Who cares about me!"

"Did you see Artie?" Donna asked.

"What a mess things are. Don't worry, the Colombians didn't see me, or if they did they didn't recognize me, we were just too busy. A couple of them got burned while trying to fight the fire; I think one of them is dead. The tree fell on him. We pulled it down. The neighbors did. While it was burning. We threw earth on the branches and some people had buckets. They're still stamping out sparks."

Marci paused for breath. "The fire's under control. I heard someone say we won't need the helicopters. Your cabin is a mess, though." This last remark was directed at Donna. Below us a few flashlights could be seen waving on and off like fireflies; acrid smoke continued to stream upward, the raging fire that had been burning fiercely just a few minutes earlier had been extinguished.

"Did you see Artie?" Donna asked a second time.

She began to cry. Greg was clearly fighting tears himself, but he put an arm around his mother and gave her a brief hug. I put one arm about his shoulders, the other around Donna's waist, and started walking uphill. She pushed my arm away irritably. "Can't you see Greg's upset!" A moment later, recognizing that she had to be upset and tired herself, she reached up and kissed me on the cheek. This time, when I held my hand out to her, Donna took it along with Greg's and followed meekly up the path.

"Did they find what they were looking for?" she whispered as we walked along. I shook my head though I'd really no idea if they had or if they hadn't and she lapsed once again into silence. Below and behind us, the remaining Colombians had begun to make slow progress upward. We increased our pace.

A streetlight marked our arrival at the top of the path where the noises of the city—the steady hum of a power transformer, automated sprinklers, a barking dog–replaced the sounds of the crickets. We found our car, slipped quickly inside. For an instant, the roar of the Volvo's engine seemed to fill the air. Girl ran the wipers, trying to wash away the small particles of soot that had settled on the windshield. Then, we started down the hill.

The ride home was a quiet one, at least in the front where Girl and I sat. I no longer knew how I felt about Marci, or how I could express what I was feeling. In the back seat, Donna and her son talked for a short while—after they consoled one another, they realized, I think, how much they gained in having each other to love—but they, too, had fallen silent by the time we pulled into my carport.

"You'd better stay with us tonight," I said.

"But Greg's schoolbooks," Donna protested.

"In the morning. We'll pick them up in the morning. Right now, we don't know whether or not Carlos and Armando know where you two live. Your husband may have told them. If they do know, and if they haven't found the dope, they'll trash your home looking for it tonight. If they don't, or if they've got what they want, then you're probably safe indefinitely.

"Now you go off with Marci." I told Donna as Girl started down the path, "Greg can stay with me."

"I'd like to be with Greg."

"Where would you sleep? I'm going to put Greg on the couch in the living room."

"I'll find someplace," Donna said.

This ambiguity in our sleeping arrangements still gnawed at me when I went in to take my shower. Donna and her son were talking intently in the living room, and I took my bathrobe in with me to avoid any possible awkwardness.

My shower completed, Donna asked, with many unnecessary apologies, whether Greg might take one. I made sure he was given and used a washcloth and was sitting on my bed waiting for the traffic to die down, when she tiptoed in a second time and asked whether she might borrow a bathrobe, along with the towels, wash clothes, and disposable razor I handed her. She had learned, watching Girl I imagine, that a touch on my arm often served as well as words, and a brief and welcome hug conveyed her gratitude.

The lights were out in the living room, and Greg's breathing could be heard slow and regular, when I finally slipped under the covers. I wondered again where Donna would sleep. I wanted her next to me and had to fight against the images that formed over and over in my mind.

The water in the bathroom showered on and on. I played a portion of Carpenter *Gothic, my* current book on tape, but soon turned it off again. The dialog was hard enough to follow at the best of times.

The sound of the pouring water stopped. She was out of the tub, bare feet on the tile floor, rough towels against her smooth skin. The bathroom door opened, the fan went off. I heard the sound of the door to the living room closing, and relaxed for the first time, only to hear the sound of her footsteps as they brought her to my bedside.

Weight of a body beside me, warm hip against mine. I let my arm slide down against her shoulder, felt the towel she was wearing about her hair against my chest. Her warm tongue reached out and licked my nipple and I went rigid in an instant.

When she was through with the one nipple, she leaned over me and gently stroked the other, gliding her warm lips down across my belly when she finished. My hands reached out of their own accord to stroke her hair. She grasped my penis, first with her fingers and then with her mouth, long full

103

lips that engulfed me completely. Shifting her position, she allowed her nipples to trail across the sensitive insides of my thighs; her own furry crotch was astride my knee and she moved back and forth rubbing against it.

When she released me, her own nipple thrust against and through my lips. I sucked eagerly and tilted my pelvis to accept and penetrate her warmth. Well lubricated, she slid down easily, and yet, at the same time, it was like threading an unyielding needle through those slender hips.

Pinning my wrists with her hands, she thrust her weight against me, her breast forcing its way after the nipple into my mouth. She began to slide up and down on my penis giving little moans of pleasure. I tried to hold back, let her finish, thought about computers, car rides, female police officers; Donna came, I bucked upwards lifting my buttocks and Donna off the bed, came and thrust raging against her, the top part of my body still pinned firmly to the mattress. And fell asleep this way with her on top of me, me inside of her.

I woke once during the night, about two or three a.m., and walked about the apartment, checking the locks on the doors and listening to the breathing of a sleeping child. To have a family of my own again, to turn back the clock, to live life with a woman I loved and who loved me, the thought filled me with an almost unbearable joy.

Returning to the bedroom, I found Donna sitting up in bed, unwinding the towel. "I've been thinking," she said, "If we could just find the money. I'm sure Artie must have hidden it somewhere in that cabin. If we found it, we could use it to pay for Greg's college education.

"Would you mind?" Her hand reached out and stroked my flank. "If we didn't return the money, I mean."

"I think that would be a great idea."

She purred, cuddled close to me and in a minute was fast asleep. I put my arms around her from behind, cupped her breasts, buried my nostrils in her now-exposed hair, and fell asleep in a field filled with sunflowers.

Chapter 26

We talked again the next morning while Donna was getting dressed. "How much can you see?" she asked, "I know you're not totally blind."

"Silhouettes, shapes. I can tell if it's light or dark, though sometimes everything seems to flicker."

"Can you see me?" she asked. I knew she was posing.

"I can tell you're a girl," I said, though this was more by scent than sight; her silhouette was really just a shapeless blob and not even that except when she posed as she did now in front of the window. "Maybe, if you moved closer," I suggested. "Let me just feel these contours." I reached out from my sitting position on the bed and touched her waist. She wasn't wearing panties. Slowly, I ran my hand up her flat belly and out along her breast. Small, hard, very feminine. "You're really built."

My other hand went exploring in the warm cleft between her legs.

"Oh, my God," she said. I put my hands behind her hips and pulled her toward me, down onto my lap. "Oh my God," she said a second time, as I penetrated deep inside her, and then, "Oh Shit." She jumped up as if she'd been stung. "I've got to get to work; Greg's got to get school."

"I'm still stiff," I said, pointing out what must have been obvious to any sighted person.

"Tonight," she said, "we'll do it tonight. After we get back from the cabin."

"In the cabin," I said, but she was already dashing about the room retrieving her clothes.

Donna declined offers of breakfast, but both Greg and I had mouths full of apple and peanut butter when Girl came to fetch us.

"You look especially spiffy this morning," Girl said, which may have been because Donna had laid out an outfit for me with, as she said, colors that really matched.

We decided I would make the initial entry into Donna's home in the event of any lurking Colombians. Girl in her jogging suit made a preliminary recognizance through the windows while we waited in the car. "Looks great, nothing seems disturbed," she said to Donna, "I guess they don't know where you live. I like your couch, by the way."

I left the automobile as they were discussing purchasing plans and options for the deluxe model sofa and made my way slowly and carefully down the block to Donna's home. Daisies formed a border along the walkway giving way to impatiens and azaleas in the shade.

The Clark home was sweet smelling, much like Donna herself. The house was a small one; the kid had his own room, not quite so fresh and clean as the others, but he had to share a nylon-strewn bathroom with his mother. I moved carefully through each room, opening closets and probing with my cane. I had only one bad moment when Donna and the others, whom I'd thought were still in the car, came crowding into the house in back of me. The sound of their footsteps left me momentarily weak and trembling. I waited, cane at the ready. Only Girl's "Boss it's us," saved me from embarrassment.

We didn't get to stand around long; Donna and Greg just had too much to do to get ready. I didn't get even the hoped-for press of the lips from Donna before they had to leave.

On the ride back, I told Girl about Donna's whispered plan for the recovery of the money. "That woman has a lot of respect for me."

Girl snorted, "And a great bod if you like skinny women. How was she by the way?"

I blushed. "What do you mean how was she?"

"Boss, you're not your usual bitchy self. Okay. You were whistling when you came out of your apartment this morning and you didn't give me 900 different reasons why the entry into Donna's house was doomed to failure. Let's face it, you finally had your ashes hauled and you'll be okay for another week or so."

I grinned, "Two days max."

Girl whooped with laughter and pounded her fist on the dash. Then she turned serious, "Tell me again how you found Donna."

I thought back to the evening before. "She was sitting in a corner of the kitchen tied to a chair. You must have seen that through the window."

"I didn't see anything; it was pitch black under the trees. Tell me what you saw, felt, touched."

"Okay." And suddenly, I was back in the cabin, a slightly musty odor, damp, the scent of trees replaced by kitchen smells: pepper, and someone had cooked eggs. I wasn't alone. "Donna," I called and heard a muffled reply. I tracked the voice to a corner near a window by a stove. I felt her hair, the smooth curve of her ear, her shoulder. A gag had been tied around her mouth, biting into the corners. I undid the knot. "Professor?" Donna's warm soprano voice.

"I believe we had a date this evening." My own deep baritone in return.

"How did she sound?" Girl's voice brought me back to the present. "Was she frightened? Had she been harmed?"

I turned to Girl. "She was scared. She hadn't been harmed. Her voice wasn't dry or choked up or anything."

"She'd been getting water?"

"Probably."

Donna's hands were tied to the back of the chair; I undid the knots. She started to rub her wrists and I said, no, let me do it.

"Fresh knots?"

"No, her hands must have been tied like that all day. I could feel the grooves where the cord had cut into her wrists."

"One rope or two?"

"I don't understand?"

"Had her wrists been tied separately to the rungs or was just a single rope thrown over the chair back?"

I thought myself back to the cabin again, heard the end of the rope hitting the floor when I undid the first knot, and then the entire rope collapsing when I finished with the second. "One rope."

"And the gag, was it freshly tied or had it she worn it all day as well?"

My fingers had traced the corners of Donna's lips not once but several times in the cabin and later as we stood by the car. "Fresh. Artie must have put the gag on just before he came back up the path."

"Or she tied it herself, just like she threw the rope over the back of the chair."

"What are you saying?"

"Boss, you're clumsy; you can't see what you're doing, yet you got those knots untied in less than a minute. She was free almost before we followed you into the kitchen. I say Donna tied herself up."

"But why?"

"So if somebody found her, the Colombians, Lionel, anyone, she could still pretend she didn't know anything, blame it all on Artie."

"Then she knows where the drugs are."

"You got it, Boss."

Chapter 27

We decided to pay a second visit to Donna's neighbors. I changed into my gray outfit—gray frock coat, soft gray trousers, and to top it off a gray homburg.

"Boss, you look ridiculous."

"Why?" My question was at least half serious.

"Well, for one thing, no one in Southern California wears a hat." She gave my homburg a flick with her fingers.

I ignored her and twirled about in the manner of a male model. "I think your Mrs. Hansen will appreciate it. Hand me my malachite cane will you? Oh, and be sure we take my walking shorts and surfing shirt along in the car, I don't intend to be wearing these hot clothes all day."

Outside Mrs. Hansen's door, we parted, me to visit the pit bull and Girl to call on her old friend. "But I thought you were dressing up so I could introduce you?" Girl said.

"On the contrary, I dressed up so that Mrs. Hansen might admire me through her window."

Girl halted for an instant on the steps leading up to Mrs. Hansen's door, braced herself to reply, but at the last moment merely giggled. I could hear her heels tapping as she walked up to Mrs. Hansen's door.

Mrs. Hansen had some delightful roses in her front garden along with some quite fragrant chrysanthemums. Girl told me later that the interior ledges, all but the ones in front of Mrs. Hansen's window on the world, were lined with houseplants. The Hansen's next-door neighbors, the hairy man and his pit bull wife, contented themselves with a row of store-bought peonies and a cherry tomato in a pot.

As I'd anticipated, my fashionable attire fairly took the pit bull's breath away. At least, she seemed somewhat calmer than the description of her Girl had provided.

I answered the hesitant, almost angry "yes" with which she answered the bell with a forceful, "We'll need your cooperation," and stepped inside her door. "Do you want to come in?" followed from her automatically as I'd expected it would.

The front hallway was an obstacle course. No help for the visually impaired here. I collided almost immediately with one of those trivet racks designed to hold small toy dogs, Toby mugs, and souvenir plates from Yellowstone National Park.

"Oh be careful, please." The soft, small hand that took my arm was in marked contrast to the cigarette-ruined voice of its owner. Gradually, the picture formed in my mind of a barrel-chested woman in her mid-forties. She had once been slim, and attractive, if not beautiful with, let us suppose, gorgeous curly blond hair. But the weight she'd added during pregnancy had never left her upper body, and only her thin short legs remained as reminders of what she once had been.

We moved slowly—as much a voyage of discovery for her as it was for me—among an amazing assemblage of small tables and cabinets. Despite her aid, I slammed my tibia against a low glass table almost the instant she sat me down in a comfortable armchair. I could hear a glass and ashtray clatter together on the table before me.

She took a seat nearby on a couch at right angles to the table and seemed on the whole pleased she had a visitor. Again, I suspect it was my costume that inspired such hopeful anticipation.

I let the silence grow. She took a cigarette out of a package, tapped it on the table and put it back in the package again. "I guess you are from the school board."

A strange assumption; could that really be her greatest fear?

"I was rather hoping," I began, "that you might tell us a little about the woman across the street."

Her breath was a mixture of orange juice and vodka as was, I suspect, the contents of her glass upon the table. "Donna Clark?"

I tapped the back of one hand with the fingers of the other to indicate assent.

"Well, I don't know. What is your interest?" Her voice had hardened, and the venom Girl spoke of had crept into the softness. "If you're with that young hussy that was here yesterday, and I don't see how you could be, you'll get no information out of us whatever."

We have ways of making you talk. Aloud, I said, "An affair between an older woman and a young school boy is a bit unusual."

Her "Oh, my God" was followed by a quick intake of breath. She reached for her glass, knocked it over, fumbled, and then licked at the few remaining drops before she went into the kitchen for a towel.

I could hear her pouring herself another drink. "Would you like something," she called, having recovered some of her poise midway through the glass, and added with alcohol-renewed courage, "He, that is, Peter is awfully mature for his age."

I was not sympathetic. "We've the matter of the two families to consider. His family and your family."

Her second, "Oh my God," when she returned to the living room was followed by a, "You have an awfully deep voice." Amazingly, she giggled.

"It's lonely sometimes," she said. "We only have the one child, he's in school, and Bill, Big Bill won't let me work."

She had moved close enough to me on the couch by this time that I could smell her perfume to say nothing of the orange juice and vodka. She waved her hand in front of my eyes. I can always tell when they do that, testing to see if I am truly blind.

"You... you don't want me to see him any more. I didn't intend to after the first time." She started to get up, banged her knees on the glass of the table and sat down again. "You're not from the school board. You're not going to tell them. Please."

She moved still closer, slipping off the couch to go down on her knees. "I'll do you if you want me to."

A not unattractive offer, even if the voice was a bit gravelly, the body still a complete unknown. But I had more pressing business, to say nothing of the questions Girl would ask if I lingered too long upon my errand.

"Just tell me who has gone in and out across the street today."

The pit bull sat back upright on the couch again and smoothed her housedress. "That tramp came back this morning with her kid and some other people. And then, about an hour after they left, that funny little man showed up with a very attractive woman."

"Tell me about them."

"He dresses like a Reverend and looks like a rat." She paused to see what effect this would have on me, but I remained impassive. (I would have to wear this gray outfit more often; a poker face is not normally one of my assets.)

"I can't see what she sees in him." the pit bull continued. "I mean he's around all the time."

"He's her Reverend." So much for my impassive demeanor. It appeared negative comments about Donna still upset me. Obviously, my infatuation was not over. It would never be over. She was so gifted, so very loving. Just recalling the sound of her laughter, the slight lilt of Tennessee in her voice made me feel happy and special.

The gravelly sound of the pit bull's voice brought me back to reality: "I didn't know it was her minister. I... I just assumed. To be honest I really don't know much about her."

No, you don't know much about anyone. You sit here in a private world of your own; you smoke, you drink and you try to get through the day.

"What about the woman?" I asked. "The one who was with the Reverend."

"Oh, I don't know, she was at least a head taller than he was. Attractive, I guess. She had on a gray skirt and a white blouse, long legs. Very conservative."

Could be anyone, I thought, and stood up preparing to leave.

"You're going to stay aren't you?" Her voice held a note of panic, a not-so-hidden plea for affection. But I had already turned toward the front hallway and she had to rush to save her precious objects from destruction. At the door, she asked, "You won't tell my husband about Peter will you? You're not from the school or anything."

"I won't tell," I said, though I felt exposure was inevitable, her husband and the school the least of her troubles.

Outside on the pathway, Girl and I exchanged findings, with Girl, of course, providing considerably more detail.

Mrs. Hansen had seen us come by that morning, though she'd not recognized me due to the change in costume. No, no one had come by the previous night, especially not the Colombians. She'd seen the Reverend. ("I wonder if that tall woman with him was your girl friend from the parking lot?") And recognized him as the visitor of the previous week.

In turn, I told Girl about the pit bull's revelations. "She's a sad case," I said.

"Right, she feels sorry for herself."

We do make our own lives; in the end, have only ourselves to blame. I didn't share with Girl my newly discovered

114

knowledge of the depth of my feelings for Donna. I didn't care if Donna were a thief or a dope-dealer or something worse. I loved her, wanted her to be mine.

In only a few hours, I would meet her in her cabin. But as to what I would say, how I'd behave, or what, in the end, I would decide to do, I hadn't the faintest idea.

Chapter 28

I had Marci drop me off at the head of the jeep trail that afternoon. "Anyone else here?" I asked, "I mean any other parked cars?"

She replied in the negative. "Sure you don't want me to come with you?" she began.

I shook my head. "I want to meet Donna alone. You can go home if you want to. I'll call a taxi when I'm through. Or, if you insist on staying, just park around the curve on a side street out of sight."

"Boss."

"I'm going," I called back over my shoulder and started down the path.

"Boss," she said, breathing heavily when she caught up with me. "You don't have a phone, so you can't call a taxi, and just what were you planning to do with her once you'd caught her?"

"Nothing. If you love someone you don't try to change them. I'll just make sure the money goes for what she said it was going to go for."

"Oh, Boss." Marci's arms circled me, gave me a hug.

The journey downward was no easier than it had been the night before. Cracks remained to be stumbled on, and loose pebbles to be tripped over. If rattlers or lizards were sunning themselves on the path that warm afternoon, they scattered at the tapping of my cane.

The air in the canyon smelled of ripe plums and the canyon jays and finches chased through the trees. Closer to the cabin, I was conscious of the odor of burnt wood, of the fire that had burned here out of control the night before.

I entered the cabin confidently, knowing I had beaten Donna here. A big mistake. People were already inside. I smelled gardenias, along with the stronger aroma of the charred furnishings, but it wasn't my Christian friend who spoke. "I might have known, the head dope fiend himself," came the Reverend's sour tones.

"Not exactly," I began, wondering what foolishness had possessed me when I'd sent Girl home.

"It doesn't matter, we've already found the drugs," said the Reverend, tapping his fingers against the counter. "Now, the question is what we're going to do with you."

Agitated, thinking as he spoke, the Reverend moved restlessly about the kitchen, tapping his fingers on every exposed surface. "Your presence creates problems (tap, step, tap). So much extra effort." He sighed deeply, then clicked his heels exultantly. I had a feeling that maybe, just maybe, he'd been dipping into the product.

My parking-lot friend, too, seemed agitated. The odd giggle punctuated her perorations. "You're a very bad man, you know (giggle). The Reverend and I had to look for a very long time to find what you hid."

"Shut up Diane," the Reverend interrupted. "Women are such weak vessels, don't you think Professor."

I offered no opinion. But the relative merits of the two sexes wasn't his main concern.

"Where is the money?" he demanded abruptly.

"I don't know."

"Don't hit him, he's blind." Diane's well-meant warning was to cause us both a great deal of aggravation later. My hand had gone up automatically to trap his wrist and, when the expected slap failed to materialize, it was left dangling for an instant in the air.

"So you know karate. Well, I'll just have to be more careful."

I heard his footsteps moving away, then a faint sound as the kitchen table shifted; he had lifted something, a bag perhaps, and unsnapped the catches.

"How's your hearing, Professor?"

"Couldn't be better."

"What's this sound?"

I didn't need Diane's frightened exclamation to tell me he'd just slammed a new load into an automatic pistol.

"Now, take off your pants. I don't really want you going anywhere."

The man had unexpected interests. No problem. If he thought doing a Lady Godiva would bother me in escaping he was dead wrong.

The gratifying gasp from Diane as I undressed was louder than it had been for the gun.

"I'd like you to sit down while I tie you. Diane, bring Professor Anders a chair." The Reverend's tone was reasonable and quite, quite mad. But I'd thought that back at the rectory.

"I'm afraid I'm going to have to tie you up, too, Diane."

"But why?" she begged.

The Reverend didn't answer, possibly because the only obvious reply was that he planned to take the cocaine and run.

The next moment, Diane had been plopped into my lap, her plump thighs around my waist and the Reverend was tying the two of us to the chair back. From the large firm breasts pressing against my chest, I gathered Marci had been correct in her initial assessment of our Christian friend. This weak, fragile vessel was built.

"You got us into this," she hissed, and I thought for a moment she was going to spit on my cheek. She was wearing much too much perfume and, as always, her reasoning was way off base.

"He's *your* minister," I retorted.

"Shut up both of you," the Reverend said. "I think I may just have to tie this rope a little tighter. No, perhaps a second one, here." And he began walking around the two of us.

"What are you doing?" Diane demanded. I sensed she might be coming down off her afternoon high.

"Merely removing your brassiere, my dear. Its absence may help to keep Professor Anders occupied while I make final preparations for your disposal."

He was right; I should have been able to work myself loose under normal circumstances, but for the expected reasons I couldn't concentrate: Diane's large nipples were against my shirtfront and the cleft in her panties pressed firmly against my own crotch.

The door opened then closed. A moment later, we could hear what sounded like digging, the sound of dirt being tossed aside and the occasional jar as shovel met rock. The blue jays were silent, no friendly little birds a la Disney to run and bring the woodsman to our rescue.

Propinquity breeds. Anyway, Diane was starting to get friendly, a little late in the day, perhaps.

"You're a good dancer. Did you know that? I think I told you the other evening. I've seen you dancing at In Cahoots, too."

Was this girl coming on to me? "I thought you were married."

She simpered or would have if the ropes and our proximity had not restrained her. "I'm not married. I mean I am but I'm not."

I gave her a sour look trying to suggest that if she kept quiet, and the Reverend didn't kill us, we might, just might, have a pleasant afternoon.

But no, she wanted to talk, a product of panic, guilt, and, as I shortly discovered, something else. "I thought I wasn't married because I'd gotten a divorce and was starting to go dancing, and smoke and have a good time, but then the Reverend convinced me I was still married in the eyes of the Lord."

"The Reverend is a coward and a thief."

"Well, yes, I mean I know it's all foolishness, but I still think Christianity has a lot to teach us. We can be nice to each other just as you said." A long pause followed in which I had the impression she was deliberately pressing her most intimate parts against me. "Will you dance with me when this is all over?"

I had an incredible erection and was speculating on what she meant by dancing, when the door to the cabin opened behind us. The Reverend?

"Can't leave you alone for an instant," Girl said, "and you have your arms around another one."

"Be careful," I admonished, "the Reverend is running around loose."

"Yes be careful," Diane echoed.

The cabin door slammed a second time. "I see one of those vile creatures wasn't enough for you." The Reverend had returned.

"He has a gun," I said needlessly, for Marci had already stepped back from the crouching position in which she'd been untying our knots and moved across the cabin floor under the Reverend's unwavering direction.

"You going to tie her up, too?" I snarled.

"That won't be necessary. My preparations outside are complete."

I didn't like the sound of that. Enough was enough. I stood up like the strong man in the Cirque de Soleil lifting the chair's weight as well as Diane's. I don't know what my intentions were, whether I thought I might slam the chair back into the Reverend forcing him to drop the gun, but I immediately toppled forward to fall with Diane beneath me.

Her panties popped, splitting across the front. As I penetrated her for the first time, her thighs locked about me convulsively.

We had no real time to enjoy ourselves when the Reverend's gun went off. Maybe he was angry we wanted to leave him. Maybe, he just didn't care for sex in public. Whatever, he missed.

Marci didn't give him a second opportunity. The instant he turned in response to the noise of our fall, she pounced.

I asked her later what hold she'd used on him; one learns in Aikido by emulating one's superiors. "I didn't use any hold, you dick. I kicked him in the spine."

# Chapter 29

After Marci finished tying up the Reverend—I'd had her gag him first, I didn't intend to listen to his self-serving bullshit any longer than I had to—she got around, finally, to releasing Diane and I.

Diane gave me a last affectionate kiss before hoisting herself to her feet. While she re-hooked and adjusted her brassiere, I struggled, manfully, to put on my walking shorts; somehow, they'd gotten twisted into a ball. The two women watched intently, occasionally laughing.

To distract them, I suggested we might clean up the place; this only sent them off into further gales of merriment. "Boss, this house is a shambles. Those Colombians literally knocked holes in the walls. Pieces of furniture are scattered all over the outer room. They're what they started to build the fire with. The kitchen's okay, but that's only because they threw all the dishes out the windows."

"We'll clean up the kitchen then," I said as frostily as I could manage, but my mind was already several hours in the future, wondering how it would be when Donna got to the cabin.

In contrast to the subtle tensions that had existed between Marci and Donna, she and Diane, instant friends, chatted away gaily as we worked. Neither noticed the shadow that passed briefly across each of the cabin's windows, a reminder, I thought, that our troubles were not yet over.

Marci described her growing impatience as she waited for me in the car, followed by her slow, almost lackadaisical walk down the jeep trail after she'd determined to rejoin me. "I was enjoying the sunshine, listening to the birds, and then, twenty seconds after I finally found you, realized I'd totally blown it."

Diane, in turn, told of her growing feeling of unease in the Reverend's company, her relief when she'd seen me walk into the cabin. (I didn't quite remember Diane reacting that way, almost the opposite, in fact, but said nothing to contradict her. I did not want to discourage what might still turn out to be a good thing.)

The Reverend had come to her earlier that day and asked her to drive him to the canyon. "I'd just got the kids off to school, when he came over talking about drugs and dope deals and how we needed to rescue Donna from herself."

The drive had taken longer than she expected, not including the initial visit to Donna's home, but the Reverend, as always, was good company, giving her plenty of advice and gloom. And when she tired of hearing her way of life being put down, "Well, here were all these beautiful houses, just like what I'd always wanted for my family. I mean when Ralph and I were married.

"We passed a lake along the way. Did you see it? Wouldn't it be lovely to live near a lake, to take the kids walking and feed the ducks. I'd like to get a house here someday. If I was married that is." This last remark brought on another chorus of laughter from the two women.

Diane had driven down into the canyon, parked and then walked with the Reverend along the streambed beneath the trees until they reached Donna's cabin.

"On the jeep trail?" Marci questioned; Diane's description of her walk had puzzled me, too. No, Diane said, a completely good road led down at the other end of the canyon. In other words, following Artie's directions the night before, risking our limbs on the uneven terrain and stumbling through the under brush, had been a totally unnecessary, potentially dangerous waste of time.

"It was a beautiful walk," Diane repeated, as if somehow the memory of the walk along the canyon floor between and among the trees enabled her to forget all the unpleasantness that had happened that afternoon, all the problems we had yet to deal with.

The one bad moment came when she and the Reverend discovered Artie Clark's body lying in the dirt where the Colombians had left it outside the cabin door. He had bites, she said, and holes in his clothes where the birds had poked him with their beaks.

They'd dug a grave; the Reverend had insisted on it; the two of them taking turns with the shovel to make sure the grave was deep enough and wide enough. She berated herself for not having done enough of the digging, but it sounded to me as if the Reverend had already been planning ahead for future corpses. Clearly, Diane hadn't figured this out yet. I hoped she never would.

The two of them had searched the cabin looking for the money, though the rooms had obviously been torn apart already by the furious Colombians.

"What about the drugs?" Marci asked, her clear voice still as reassuring and invigorating for me as it had been the moment I heard her speak after the gun went off and knew, thankfully, I was still alive.

It seemed the Reverend had found the drugs right away, wrapped in a large baggie hidden beneath the propane tank. "As if he already knew where they were," Marci interjected, putting both our thoughts into words.

Their search for the money had not met with success. Discouraged (Diane), irritated (the Reverend), they had decided to wait for Donna or whoever next came along. While waiting, the Reverend had opened the baggie to show her the evil powder, had even made her sniff some to show how foul the stuff was, and the rest was history.

A branch snapped against the rooftop, rousing us from our reverie, and we heard a small bird or animal scurry through the underbrush. The shadow passed across the windows a second time.

"Help me move the Reverend out of sight," I said to Marci. "Afterward, I want you to walk Diane back to her car. She can drive you to yours."

"Then I'll come back here." Marci replied eagerly.

I was wrong; I knew I was wrong, but I had as little choice over what I said next as to whether I took my next breath, "No, you go home. This time, I've got to handle things alone." As they walked off, the shadow moved again across my window and someone stumbled against a leaf-covered log.

I sat in the chair where Donna had been sitting the evening before trying to regain some of the inner calm that allows us to act on reason, not impulse. I'd loved her once; I could love her still.

A timid rap on the door, Donna's footsteps, the smell of her perfume as she put her arms about me and kissed me on the cheek. I reached for her breast, kissed her full on the lips. "Are you all right?" she asked.

"I missed you," I said.

"I missed you, too." She turned and looked about the room, her back against my chest, safe it seemed within the circle of my arms. Apparently, the avaricious Reverend would have been as much a surprise to her as he had been to me.

"I'm sorry about your cabin."

"It's not important."

I hugged her again. She smelled so good. "I found the dope," I said, "but I couldn't find the money."

"Don't worry, I know where the money is."

I feigned surprise.

"I think I know where Artie must have hidden it." She babbled on as I heard her moving a chair—the chair she'd once tied herself to, across the kitchen floor.

"Help me a moment will you?" I stood patiently as she directed me to stand alongside the chair back. I remained slightly off balance while she reached up above her to the false ceiling and probed behind the oven fan. The bag made a scraping sound as she inched it toward her. With a final press of her hand on my shoulder for support, she clambered down again to the floor, making sure to brush my lips with her perfumed cheek.

"I found it!" Surprise, surprise. "Artie was never any good at hiding things. You can even see the marks where the panel was removed... oops... that is, the panel's edge is clear, while the rest is grease covered." So much for the Reverend's keen eyesight. "We have both the money and the cocaine now; I can do everything I've always wanted to for Greg—college, a car when he's ready."

"'Course, we'll have to turn the dope in." I put in my two cents, finally.

"Not necessarily." she said, her voice not yet sharp and angry as it would be later. She deliberately dragged the chair back into position so it squeaked on the patched linoleum floor.

"Donna, I mean, I wouldn't know how to begin to dispose of it."

"Maybe one of Artie's friends." I could tell she was improvising.

"Or the Reverend. Unless, he plans to keep it all for himself."

She hesitated only an instant before swooping down to pick up the bag. I caught her wrist before she could stand up again. We stood up together.

"Let go," she said.

"You don't want to get involved with dope."

"Greg needs the money." A familiar theme that, I have to admit, still held a lot of appeal for me.

126

"But he doesn't need to get hooked."

"Oh, the dope won't go to him." Donna sounded shocked.

"Just to other teenagers like him."

She paused without replying and then began to walk across the kitchen. I walked with her, never releasing her arm. When she attempted to shake free, I let my own arm, loose as a rag doll, shake along with hers.

She stamped her foot angrily and let the bag fall heavily against my leg. "Oh, take the dope if you want to."

But I did not reach down, if that was what she expected.

"What are you going to do with it?" she asked. She just could not let it go. I could hear her fumbling again behind the oven. The shadow passed a third time across the kitchen window.

"Burn it, I guess. Or bury it."

"Burn it!" she repeated derisively, "You'll get high from the fumes. And if you bury it, someone will just dig it up again."

"Give it to the cops."

"They'll ask too many questions. You'll have to tell them about the money."

"Mail it to the cops anonymously."

"They'll trace it to you."

She had an answer for everything. What had happened to the sweet innocent country girl smelling of sunflowers? Never had been such a person, probably. "It's love's illusions we recall. I really don't know life at all."

"Oh, just give it to me." she snapped. I could hear the sound of a pistol cocking for the second time that afternoon. "No, don't come close. I know you're a Tai Kwan Do master. Throw it to me."

I felt around on the table, then tossed her the baggie.

"I'm going to go, now," she said.

I hated to spoil the surprise but, "I don't think you'll get out of the cabin."

"You can stop bullets can you, Mr. Invincible." The contempt was evident in her voice (and all this time, I'd thought she was crazy about my dick).

"I think Lionel will want the money and the dope too, probably." The shadow that had passed across each of the windows reached the door; its owner just had to bang the door open. Startled, Donna pulled the trigger. The bullet passed by inches from my skull.

"Lionel!" Donna exclaimed, and her voice was as sweet and loving as it had been in our most intimate moment. "I've found the money you were looking for."

"What about the coke?" Lionel asked.

"That was never really part of the deal." Some of the sweetness was gone now, but still the warm tone remained, promising, it seemed, more than just drugs.

"Deal was with your husband."

"Hardly. He could never have thought up anything like this."

"I dunno," Lionel said as if it was something about which he'd need to do a great deal of thinking. She slithered against him and I could hear them both breathing heavily. I took a step toward them, hoping they were now too involved to hear me.

"Lionel," came the sweet syrupy voice again, "I don't see why we can't just divide the money from the drugs between us. Massoud doesn't have to know."

I took another step.

"We could go away together," she continued

"Greg's going to get the money for college?" the big man asked; he, too, needed reassurance.

"Not necessarily." I imagine she pressed herself against him at this point, her hands working on his pants front, "You and I might want to spend the money on something else."

The big man shifted his weight angrily. The floor of the cabin moved upward against my rising heel. "Greg's supposed to get that money."

"Oh, he will my puppy, he will. I'm so glad you understand. We just need to get rid of him."

He, you, him, what did all those pronouns mean? I regretted not being able to see their body language. Who (or whom) was I kidding? The "him" they needed to get rid of had to be me. If I could just figure out which one of them had the gun, I might be able to pull off a quick attack. Another step.

"He's a nice guy," Lionel said. Oh bless, you big fellow, but I'm really not a nice guy, you know. Step. "He likes Greg as much as I do."

"I know honey, we all like Greg."

I missed what happened next; had she gone for the gun, or his dick? She must have pissed Lionel off whatever she did, for the next thing I heard was a loud slap and the sound of Donna hitting the floor near me.

I stepped forward and placed my heel on her hand.

"You bathurd." she said, sounding as if she had a mouthful of loose teeth. Reaching up with her free hand, she clawed at my balls. Thankfully, Lionel stepped on her other arm, and we could hear the lower part of her body thrashing up and down against the floor as she tried to break away. "You bathurds; oh you bathurds."

"Let's tie her up," I said to the big man, for I couldn't stand the sound of all that thrashing, much less the thought of what Lionel's weight must be doing to the small bones of her wrist. In a moment, she was tied up and lying on the rear porch next to the Reverend. The lizards sunning themselves nearby seemed intrigued by the display.

Now for the bad news. "The money goes back to your boss, I guess."

"Not necessarily."

Lionel's answer surprised me. "We just take it and run?"

I could tell the big man had spent a fair amount of time under the trees thinking about this while he waited to see what would develop inside the cabin.

"We give Mr. Favor the cocaine. That will keep him happy. I'll tell him the exchange was already made. We can give Greg the money."

"He's just a kid." How did I get to be such a spoilsport? Lionel's idea of swapping the dope for the money really was a good one.

"We give the money to his mom, then. No, that's not such a good idea is it?" The big man scratched his head.

Oh Donna, why couldn't you have been a completely different person, the person I wanted you to be?

"Professor. You know about stocks and things. Why don't you just take the money and invest it for him... until he's old enough."

My mouth dropped open. I must have looked like a ventriloquist's dummy. "How do you know I won't run away with it?"

"You don't need money do you?"

I shook my head. I had more than enough from the insurance settlement, well, enough, anyway.

"Then just do it."

And I did do it. An Artie Clark Memorial College fund will be waiting for Greg when he graduates high school

Lionel and I met Marci coming back along the path—she'd disobeyed orders again, so the money and I went back with her, while Lionel and the dope went off to see his boss. We went back later to untie Donna and the Reverend, but they were already gone.

Miss Woo keeps calling trying to persuade me to change my mind about teaching high school. Yes, I've had sex with her. I've had sex with Brigitte, too. Diane? Well, I try to stay our of her way.

Donna moved to Glendale taking Greg with her—a second In Cahoots is in Glendale, where she can go and not have to confront me across the dance floor. It didn't really matter about the move because Marcie and I showed Greg how to use postcards. "You can phone us if your mother tells you to, but if you want to be sure your message remains private, then write to us."

He knows it's important he stay in contact. The Artie Clark Memorial College fund is waiting for him when he graduates high school next year.

Don't stop reading now: Two bonus short stories are provided on the following pages.

# To Find The Crime
by Paul Anders
Copyright 2009 by zanybooks.com

I can hear the tap. It doesn't drip often, perhaps once every five minutes. But it should be fixed. I'll speak to the landlord about it tomorrow. It's hard to get his attention. I want him to pay attention when I talk to him. I want him to do something about the tap, not laugh at me. He seems a very bitter man, pretending to laugh but really very angry.

It's awfully noisy in this building. The people next door, the mother and her two children are the worst. It's not the constant sound the children make, but the yelling they do. The sister yells at the brother; the mother yells at the daughter. They don't ever seem to speak quietly or without anger.

The elderly woman on the other side likes to think she is quiet. I have heard her often on the phone complaining about other people's noise. She is quiet herself, most of the time, until she gets on the telephone. Hard of hearing, she does not realize how loud her own voice is. And in the middle of the night, when she gets up to go to the bathroom, the sound of her flushing toilet echoes through my walls.

At the other place, it was noisy too, TV's blaring, children running up and down the halls. But I was working then and at night, when I was home, it would usually quiet down.

I made friends with some of the people there. I do not have any friends here. I'm not sure I could afford to or, if they knew about me, they would want to.

The blond girl in the corner apartment is very nice. She is quiet and considerate. I would like to speak with her but I would have to be on the walk outside at just the right moment, when she leaves for work or when she comes back home in the evening. I could wait for her downstairs but I do not want to get in the way of the other tenants. They might not understand; they would ask 'why are you just standing on the path waiting' and I would not want to tell them.

When you wake up on a Chelsea morning, you do not expect to find a flock of owls hooting from the top of a palm tree or, incredibly, a single wayward duck outside on the walkway pecking at the ants. He was here yesterday, too, and must still be looking for the park and the lake where he belongs.

What a meaningless life, half the day spent in finding your way, the other half in losing it again. Before I went blind, I had a job to go to. Now, my "job," if one can call it that, consists in placating tenants, tending my roses, and supervising the endless stream of handymen these failing apartments seem to call for. A steady income from the rents? Maybe, if I really work at it. I make almost as much from my detective agency with its two or three clients a month, four if we have a white-collar crime wave.

A burble of boiling water comes from the kitchen. The coffee machine goes on each day automatically at 7:45, otherwise as Marcie puts it, "you'd lie there all morning with no reason to get up."

"Have breakfast with me; there's motivation."

"No time this semester. I've a nine o'clock class."

And just what does she do, I wonder, between seven a.m. and nine?

I went for a short walk; by now, most of the people in the surrounding apartments are at work or at school. I do not want to meet or talk with other people and, as I'd hoped, encountered almost no one on my way.

Once a woman with a baby carriage waved to me. She raised one of her child's hands and had him wave to me also, so I waved back.

My landlord was up when I returned, on his hands and knees in the center of the walkway. He is blind and perhaps does not realize he is blocking the path. "Good morning."

"Good morning, uh ..."

"John."

"Good morning, John."

"Good morning." I do not know what else to say. He is looking up in my direction with a puzzled almost commiserating expression. Perhaps, he thinks I'm slow witted.

"Your roses are beautiful."

"Thanks."

"I like the way they smell." What a stupid thing for me to say.

"I like the way they smell, too. They were chosen for their fragrance. This one is called Glamis Castle. Smell it; what does it remind you of?"

"Spice."

He grunts at my answer, not entirely pleased. "Well, it's early days. You'll smell more as the blooms begin to open."

"How is...? I mean, how are...? How goes?" I am not sure what I'm asking. He is still kneeling in the center of the path and I cannot get by until he moves.

"The detective agency? I'm on guard again this afternoon from two to four when school lets out. Otherwise, things are real slow."

"You're a detective?"

I have offended him. He stands up in the middle of the path, hand outstretched still holding the rose clippers and looks at me. He can't really be looking at me; he is blind. I try to squeeze past him but he is already lecturing.

"Blind men have hands and feet just like other people. And friends they can call on when they need assistance. They can listen. My computer talks to me, so does my tape recorder.

"Blind men have brains." He points to his head. "I can put one and one together and get two. If a crime were to be committed in the building, I'd examine the clues, combine the information with what I already know from practical experience and track down the culprit."

He pauses, for once having expressed his anger. I reply, careless of what I am saying, "What if you knew someone had committed a crime, but you didn't know what he'd done or who might be looking for him." The words come leaping from my mouth. I bite down, try to swallow them back.

"That would be tough. It's a lot easier when you can start with the crime and follow the clues."

What if you knew someone had committed a crime, but not what crime he'd committed? I'd be the last person in the world to figure it out. I've never been the type who memorized faces on wanted posters or faithfully sat through America's Most Wanted. And I wasn't about to go down to the post office and ask someone to describe the faces to me, now.

A tape of an escaped criminal's voice would help, as would a knowledge of his or her habits, favorite brand of soap, hair spray, and shaving lotion. As I told John, it's a lot easier to start with the clues and work forward to the criminal.

Oh, and I could call Agnes, my policewoman friend if I really needed to track someone down. I could call her, that is, if I wasn't afraid of starting things up all over again.

I don't think my newest tenant was just making conversation. He is guilty of something, even if it's only having impure thoughts. Odd, anyway you look at it. When Marcie gets back, I'll ask for her opinion.

I shouldn't have confided in Mr. Anders. Something about the way he talked to me made me feel I was free to speak to him. This is the way the police break you down; they let you think they're your friend, then snap the cuffs on once they've got your confession.

Mr. Anders said he was a detective. All right, Mr. Hotshot blind detective, figure it out on your own. You won't get any more help from me.

I always get hungry when I'm nervous. Though it was only eleven o'clock in the morning, I opened another can of sardines and finished the rolls I'd bought the previous day. I made a decision at the same time. I would avoid Mr. Anders altogether if I could, not give him another chance to worm information out from me.

There was still the matter of the tap.  One drop every five minutes, no, four and a half minutes now, I've timed it.  The drops fall faster as the crack in the washer opens.  The best thing is to fix it myself.  Tomorrow, I'll purchase a screwdriver and a set of washers.  I'll just have to live with the sound till then.

When Marcie returned from school, I discussed my theory and tried to get from her a better idea of what John was like. "Strange, weird, even creepy," were the first, not unexpected words out of her mouth.  "When you run into him on the stairs or on the walkway, he makes such a fuss about getting out of your way that you're almost tempted to run him over just to see how he would react."

"Do you think he could be guilty of some crime?"

"Depends on the crime.  Armed robbery, no.  Exposing himself in the shrubbery, maybe.  Why do you ask?"

"I think he may have committed a crime somewhere else, that he's here hiding out from the law."

"These apartments of yours are a great location for a hideout, Boss.  Maybe you should put that in your ad the next time there's a vacancy."

He and the tall woman ate supper together.  I forgot to mention her before.  She's very attractive; not the sort that would ever notice me. I've watched her as she does her evening run; she'll go by on the sidewalk only a few inches away and not even notice I am there.

She helps Mr. Anders, I think.  Drives his car
when he needs to go somewhere.

I could find out from her if he really is a
detective.


The next morning, John's strange confession still nagged at me.  He
was guilty of something, but what?

I put on a tape of the last Green Umbrella concert letting the
textures of Iatiku fill the room.  Hopefully, the music might help me
to think.  The composer, Ruth Loman, said Iatiku was based on Zuni
ceremonials.  I wondered how long the Zuni had been using
harpsichord, marimba, and bass clarinet as adjuncts to their worship.

I wasn't thinking clearly at all.  If I wanted help tracing a criminal
to his crime, I needed to call Agnes.  She's a lieutenant now in the
Huntington Beach police and has access to all the information I need.
She's looked at all the wanted posters.  I could invite her here for
supper and let her look at John.  But I couldn't, not without making
that final, irrevocable commitment.  "The next time I stay the night it
will be as your wife; marry me or let me go."

The music switched to Ben Johnston's Invocation.  The voice of
the soprano cut through the dissonance created by oboe, bassoon,
and trumpet, overcame the strings.  "Many know the surface of this
ocean, but they understand nothing of the depths."

My tenant files are located in a set of folders adjacent to my roll
top desk.  I sifted through them, looking for the card John had
completed.  I could have waited for Marcie to read it for me--it would
have made a good deal more sense, but I just wanted a general
impression.  By holding the card up in the light from the open
doorway and putting it out to the side almost at a level with my left
eye, I could at least see if he'd filled it out completely.

The space for the address of his last residence had been
scratched out once then written over, smeared might be a better

138

word.  Why was I not surprised?  He'd almost gone through he paper on his second attempt. It made no difference.  What he'd written was still unreadable without Marcie's aid.

I wasn't alone in my apartment.  A shadow had entered by the front door and walked four, no five steps into my living room. Unperturbed, I walked around the partition into the kitchen, and got out two cups. Half filling each with milk, I placed them in the microwave.  When they were heated, I added the already-warm coffee to each cup and carried them into the living room.  The intruder still had not spoken, though he'd taken several additional steps inside, each time pausing to look about him as if he, too, were blind and needed to get acclimated with his surroundings.

"Won't you pull up a chair John, and have some coffee?"

Can he see? Or is it true what he said the other day about having another sense, a detective's intuition that let's him fit together all the clues. Sometimes my father would pretend he didn't know about an error my mother or I had made.  She was always getting us both into trouble.  I'd smile, relieved, and walk past him, forgetting how often he stored up grudges.  He would hit out suddenly, striking me across the head or, worse, grab me by the neck and pull me close to him, his face so close to mine that we shared the same breath.

The lights went out.  It had been dark before in Mr. Anders' apartment; now there was almost no light at all. When my father shoved me in the closet, the only light would be a thin ribbon under the door.  Sometimes he would place a towel across the crack blocking out the light completely.

"No, need to panic, John. It's all right. I can see, . . . as well as I could before." Mr. Anders chuckled. "Some well-meaning neighbor must have closed the front door. I'll open it again; stay there till I do; be calm; wait." I could hear his heavy footsteps, know something of what it must be to be blind.

"You didn't spill the coffee on the rug?" His voice, irritated now, angry, was like my father's.

"It's all right," I told him. But it was not all right. The coffee had spilled down the sides of my cup. How had he known? I wiped off the drops quickly onto my shirt. I would clean up everything carefully before I left to make sure I'd left no fingerprints.

A lucky break, someone shutting the door like that. I usually keep the curtains drawn and only turn on the light when I have company. Panicked as he was, John might be willing or unwitting enough to answer questions. "So you lived in the 300 block at your last address?"

"Six hundred. No, 300, you're right."

He was trying to trap me. I must have written 300 on the card.

"In Garden Grove?"

"No, Ana ... Fullerton. I've got to go now." He turned as silently as when he'd first come in and slipped out the newly reopened door.

He knows now. He knows I'm guilty of something, but he still does not know what.

Has he gone to the police?  I heard him go out a short while ago.  When I followed him downstairs, I saw he and the tall girl get into his car. But what can he tell the police?  What crime does he think I've committed? I only wanted to talk to her.

I'd made sure to wipe my fingerprints off the coffee cup this morning.  I know now this was why he gave the cup to me.  To get my prints to show the police.  My fingerprints might be somewhere in my apartment, though I've tried to be careful, wiping up after myself as I go along.

I will go over the entire apartment now with Comet and Mr. Clean just to be sure.  I bought them when I first moved in even though Mr. Anders told me the apartment had already been cleaned.  My father insisted on cleanliness.  He would make my mother wash before they had sex and would take a shower himself, afterward.

As soon as I could get Marcie fed and out of the house we went driving off in all directions.  "You should call, Agnes," she began, but I headed her off quickly.

"I'm not going to do that.  I'm not ready to make that commitment."

"Boss." She put her hand on my arm.  Her voice was soft, gentle, almost a caress.  "You don't have to explain to me."

I felt awful.  Maybe it was time to call Agnes, to move on with my life.

The card John had completed gave his previous address as 650 Lynnthorpe.  Actually, the "thorpe" part had been written over some other street name which had been scratched out repeatedly.

The Thomas Guide offered a Lynnbrooke in Yorba Linda, a Lynwood Avenue in Orange, Lynwood Drives in Brea and Anaheim, and a Lynwood Place in Garden Grove.  No Lynnthorpe, but I hadn't really expected there would be one.

He'd written down Garden Grove on his card but Lynwood Place was up in the 13000's.  We thought Lynwood Avenue might be a winner but it came to an end well before the house numbers were low enough.  Brea and Yorba Linda were just too far away--for that evening, anyway.  By the time we reached Lynwood Drive in Anaheim, we had only the streetlights to assist us.  Again, the numbers were wrong and there wasn't a sign of homes, only warehouses closed up tight for the night.

"It's not 'Lynn' something then."

"But that's what he wrote on the card."

"Maybe Lynn is the girl he killed."

"If he killed someone."

"What about Orangethorpe?  It's the only 'thorpe' I know of."

It was the only 'thorpe' I knew of, too.

We stopped at Albertson's to pick up supplies--Egg Beaters, orange juice, one percent milk, and toilet paper, so our trip wasn't a complete waste.  We would try again the next day, first thing in the morning.

I watched from the safety of the alley and saw them unload the groceries.  I was safe then; he hadn't gone to the police.  They had been gone so long; I hadn't known whether to leave or to stay.  The girl from down the alley came back home while I was waiting.  I thought of talking to her, but she might be afraid if I suddenly appeared out of the shadows. I did not want her to run away like the other one.

She was wearing a white sweater with buttons down the front, very modest, and carried a bag of

groceries held in front of her.  Perhaps, I should
have offered to help her, but it was only a single
bag.

'First thing in the morning' meant after Marcie's nine o'clock class,
then after the appointment with her college counselor she had at
ten.  I'd toyed again with the notion of telephoning Agnes, asking her
aid in looking up a John Roberts (though this was probably a
pseudonym) and a missing, or molested, or murdered "Lynn."  But
could not bring myself to make the call.

   "Orangethorpe" Avenue was a bust.  Both the 300 and 600 blocks
were zoned commercial.  "Orange" wasn't much more satisfactory,
but there was a restaurant nearby that served dim sum.  That left
"Orangewood" to examine after lunch, those three street names one
of the few remaining clues that what was all shops and residences
today had once been acre after acre of orange groves.

   360 Orangewood was home to a small group of garden
apartments much like those I owned in Huntington Beach.  The first
person encountered, a short fat woman with a clean apron and a
dirty blouse, spoke only Spanish.  Between us, Marcie and I
established that she only came to this address to clean.  An elderly
man denied all knowledge of a Lynn or a John or even of some
terrible crime.  "I've lived here for the past sixteen years," he said,
"don't try to tell me I don't know what's going on."

   But on second thought, there had been a crime in the
neighborhood, a woman killed, a child molested.  He pointed off in
the distance.  "Which way?" I asked Marcie.

   "Could be the 600 block."  Bingo.

   It took only a minute or two to reach our next parking place.  I
had my seat belt off, car door open, and was up on the curb in
seconds.  But I didn't get the action I craved.

"Why don't you stay here, Paul. I think things would go faster if I went ahead first and asked around."

Marcie was as direct as ever. Things would go faster without a blind man tagging along.

"This apartment complex is a lot larger than the last one," she offered by way of explanation. It wasn't an apology.

"Tell me where we are then." I wasn't going to wait in the car.

"There's sort of a small park here with swings and a basketball court. Stop. You'll have to lift your leg if you want to climb over the rope fence.

"You're not going to wait, are you. Stop. Turn right; follow the path. Stop. Just behind you is a bench. You could wait there for me. Please."

I turned and sat on the bench. I banged the back of my leg against it, but I wasn't going to give her the satisfaction of knowing I was in pain. Much good my mock fortitude did me. A cheery "bye" and she'd gone galumping off.

Abandoned, I sat and listened to the birds. The starlings were angry about something, not necessarily me, a pigeon perhaps or even a hawk.

A tennis ball bounced toward me across the concrete. Three bounces and I was able to reach down a hand and retrieve it from where had come to rest against the bench. For several moments, I waited for the shout, waited so I could throw it back in the direction of the sound. Silence, although I was sure there had to be someone nearby watching.

"What's the matter?" A young boy's voice.

"He won't give me back my ball." The voice of a still younger girl.

"Hey, mister, give her back her ball. What do you want to keep it for?"

Great, now I was the bad guy. I flipped the unwanted ball underhand in the direction I hoped the kids were standing.

Apparently the little girl dropped my toss for I heard the boy say to her, "You've got to catch it like this, see."

I was out of the loop again.

"Are you blind, mister?" the young girl asked. Her voice was somewhat closer than it had been, perhaps a mere five or six steps in front of me.

"Sure am."

"I'm sorry I got upset."

"Your apology is accepted." I stood up and held out my hand. " My name is Paul. What's yours?"

"Lynn." She hadn't moved any closer so I sat down again, feeling like an idiot that I'd held my hand out.

"I'm not supposed to come near you, so I can't shake your hand. Not since the other man tried to hurt me."

Lynn. Lynnwood. Lynnthorpe. "John, you mean?"

"He hurt Sandra awfully bad. She's dead. It's not nice when you're dead even though there are angels."

I couldn't say one way or the other about the angels, though I figured I'd find out soon enough. I guess maybe blind is halfway there.

"Lynn, come away from that man." An older woman's voice, her mother perhaps, or simply a concerned neighbor. "Who are you? What are you doing here?"

"Paul Anders." I stood up again.

"He's blind," Lynn said, unnecessarily. She might have said instead, "He gave me back my ball," or "he's nice," or even, "He knows John."

"I think I know John."

"John? John Small?"

145

Marcie came back just about the time the Anaheim police arrived. They'd received half a dozen calls about me already. Not surprisingly, people in that neighborhood weren't all that keen about strangers who talked to small children. I gathered John had tried to molest Lynn, or maybe (since he was not there to defend himself) had just tried to talk with the little girl and been misunderstood. She'd panicked and cried out for help. Sandra Norman, their neighbor from two doors down, had been killed coming to Lynn's rescue. The two adults, John and Sandra, had fought, Lynn and Sandra both still screaming. The fight ended with John smashing the woman's head against the concrete (whether accidentally or on purpose wasn't clear). By that time a crowd had gathered and John knocked down another woman in his run for freedom.

He had no friends in the 600 block of Orangewood.

Of course, before I learned all this I had to explain my own presence, not that it was all that difficult once Marcie put in an appearance. While I still had everyone's attention, I told them all about John Roberts and where they could find him. There was no doubt in anyone's mind that John Roberts and John Small were the same person. The Anaheim Police Department contacted the Huntington Beach authorities as quickly as they could. But by the time they closed in on our building, John had disappeared.

The rooms are very small in my new home, small and dusty. "You're lucky I can rent you anything at all," the super told me. The rug is stained so badly that even the equipment I rented at the supermarket has no effect on it. "What did you want to do that for? The owner will just raise your rent when he finds out what you've done."

The Case of The Spilled Perfume
by Paul Anders
Copyright 2009 by zanybooks.com

When people first learn I'm a detective, they seem to fall into one of two categories, neither of which I particularly care for:

The first group exclaims, "A blind detective, no way!" Right, like I don't have a brain and couldn't hire people to do the leg work if and when I felt the need.

The second group is almost but not quite as obnoxious. "Oh, I'll bet your other senses are really developed. You can probably smell fear on a suspect." Right, which explains why the one blind guy they have a job for down at the courthouse is selling magazines instead of serving as a lie detector.

The case of the spilled perfume really illustrates the point. No, I didn't "sniff" out the solution. Blind detectives are pretty much like the sighted kind, down to and including the fact that sometimes we just get lucky.

By the way, this case isn't all that special. No corpses, no missing jewels, no real client either. It was just Mrs. Harkness, my newest and least desirable tenant demonstrating her lack of parenting skills again.

She was outside on the walkway arguing with Karen her teen-age daughter. I know, because Mrs. Wilks, my oldest and quietest tenant had phoned, not to complain, she said, as always, but because she thought the noise might disturb the other tenants.

Mrs. Harkness and her daughter Karen had indeed taken it to the streets. First had come the yelling from inside their apartment. Then the race pell-mell down the steps from the second floor with Mrs. H. screaming like a banshee all the way.  Now, they were on my walk, a definite threat to the roses as well as to the peace and tranquility of the neighborhood.

"You can just go live with your father.  See how you like that."

"Fine.  Take me there now.  I want to stay with him."

"You are totally ungrateful; if you only knew how hard I've worked to give you and your brother a home."  And so on and so forth.  I believe the technical name Transactional Analysts give to this game people play is "Uproar."  It doesn't really matter what the players say as long as there is a lot of noise and confusion.  Both parties are guaranteed a win only if they can stay angry; usually this game is followed by the equally noisy and disgusting, "I'm Sorry I Hurt Your Feelings."

The pretext for this particular return match was Karen's spilling a bottle of perfume all over her mother's dresser, that and messing with her mother's things again.  Pardon me, Karen was alleged to have spilled the bottle.

"I didn't touch it.  I never go near your stupid things."

"You're always trying on my clothes, using my lipstick. Your mother deserves her privacy, too.  It's not as if there's any room in these tiny apartments."

Now, wait just one dog-gone minute lady.  Speaking as your landlord, there is ample room in these apartments providing you don't stuff too many people in them.  As I recall our initial conversation, back when you were begging me to rent to you, it was two small children who would be living with you, not two hulking teenagers.

About this time Mrs. Harkness must have noticed that I and Marcie and two or three other tenants had gathered round as witnesses to their debate.  The strident voice vanished to be replaced by a sweet almost saccharine tone.

"See what you've done, Karen.  I told you not to make so much noise.  I'm sorry everybody.  You know how teenagers are."  Perhaps, but we also know how self-centered, self-indulgent, and hopelessly inconsistent you are, Mrs. H., a veritable recipe for parental disaster.

"You're always blaming me for everything. I tell you I didn't do it."

I can only suspect Mrs. Harkness looked about her for reassurance at this point. She didn't make eye contact with me.

"Well, who did it then?" The strident tone had returned. I could imagine the crossed arms and baleful stare.

"You should ask Professor Anders, he's a detective." The elderly Mrs. Wilks had arrived on the scene.

"Yes, Paul, you could help them." came another, equally familiar voice, that of my companion Marcie, all around factotum, friend and, in this instance, troublemaker.

I tried not to be sarcastic. "Perhaps you'd like me to take statements from everyone, where they were when the crime was committed, and so forth. I'll take the Harkness' cat, Marci, and you can interview their dog." (Which reminds me; the Harkness' aren't supposed to have either pet; pets are definitely forbidden in their lease.)

"Muffy couldn't have done it. It must have been Oscar." Did I hear sobbing or the beginnings of it?

"Oscar is with your brother."

"Why don't you blame him, then? Why do you always blame me?"

"Why don't you suspect Karen's brother, Mrs. Harkness?

"Deirdre, you can call me Deirdre."

I don't think so. Since the first month you were late with the rent—and, yes, I insisted on you paying it, our relationship has been adversarial.

"I've told my daughter a dozen times to stay away from my cosmetics."

"I didn't touch them."

149

I took charge then. It's a male thing. "Please young lady, I'll listen to you later, I promise." With a sigh that hinted at infinite sadness, Karen grew silent. A rather pleasant young woman; I doubted her mother would have given way so easily. In fact, her mother didn't. She persisted in telling the story her way rather than in the order I wanted to hear it. Reaching out a cautionary finger toward her lips, I accidentally jammed it against her nose. Sorry about that.

With tears in her voice—that blow against her nose must have smarted, Mrs. Harkness told how she'd returned home to find her bedroom reeking of perfume, and the bottle of the expensive liquid lying on its side on her dresser.

"Were there other spilled bottles?"

Nothing else had been overturned, which seemed to exonerate Muffy the cat. I'd never for an instant considered Oscar, a typically awkward dachshund, to be a serious suspect. Which left as possibilities only Karen the daughter, the brother—I didn't know his name, and a mysterious stranger who went from apartment to apartment spilling bottles of perfume.

"Is anything missing from your rooms?"

"I don't really know. I don't own anything worth stealing. I could check." She went upstairs, leaving Karen the daughter to shift insecurely from one foot to another under our gaze.

Fortunately, Karen was rescued from fatal embarrassment by the arrival of her brother with his dog. The latter quickly wound his leash about my legs. I carefully raised one foot, reached about in the direction of movement and prepared to stamp on him. Dog and leash ran in the opposite direction.

"Andy!" A returning Mrs. Harkness greeted her son.

"What happened, Momma?"

What a touching reunion. I could understand how the daughter might sometimes feel neglected. Finally, Mrs. H deigned to tell us that, no, there was nothing missing from her apartment.

"Wouldn't the one who spilled the perfume have traces of it on them?" This question, a sensible one, came from Marci.

"I don't know." Mrs. Harkness said, "The smell is so strong in my apartment, I can't be sure of anything."

"I could try to find out," Mrs. Wilks offered and soon everyone who had been part of the original group of onlookers was running about sniffing either Karen or Andy. While both children had their adherents, not surprisingly the majority of the votes went to Mrs. Harkness as she had the most recent exposure to the stuff. (Personally, I thought Mrs. H well rid of the odious liquid. What an excellent reason Mr. H. would have had for divorcing her.)

"Maybe, Paul could smell them."

What an incredibly stupid idea! And from the one person in the world I trusted. Marcie, you are out of your mind. I didn't say this aloud. I didn't say anything; I simply stood with my mouth hanging open. To think that someone I'd know for years, had known intimately, would treat me as a stereotype.

"Oh, would you Dr. Anders?"

Of course I would; your friendly neighborhood pedophile is always anxious to walk around smelling small children.

I smelled Karen first: strawberry shampoo, orange-scented nail polish, wintergreen breath. I hoped for the girl's sake she did a better job of matching her clothes.

One sniff of Andy and I knew we had a problem, though not quite the one the others had in mind. Cigarettes, coffin nails. Half a pack, at least; the aroma pervaded his clothes. Did Mrs. Harkins spend any time at all with her kids? Quietly, not wanting to embarrass him, I said. "Andy, you and I have got to have a talk." Well, somebody had to play the role of parent in that family.

"I ... I don't see how you could know. I wore gloves."

Not know? What did the kid think we did back when our parents weren't around to supervise us? I know what cigarettes smell like, even though I wouldn't be caught dead today with one in my mouth. But what did gloves have to do with it?

Marci is a tad sharper than I. "You wore gloves so the smell of the perfume wouldn't get on your hands. You wanted your sister to get the blame. You wanted your mother to send her back to live with your father so you'd have your own room."

All this time, the kid is going "yes" under his breath and crying to beat the band.

Mystery solved—blind luck on my part, that and a kid with a guilty conscience. Mrs. Harkness and her daughter are hugging. "Oh, can you ever forgive me." Andy gets a swat on his rear. Mrs. H. comes over and, though I would have settled for her shaking my hand, hugs me too and says how grateful she is. She even starts coming by when the rent isn't due, wearing that dreadful perfume and little else, to talk about how Andy ought to have a father just like me. But I was wise to her; she just wanted me to rent her family a larger apartment.